WHEN REALITY CRACKS

BY

MICHAEL DRYDEN

Caution: Not to be believed

ISBN: 978-1-7369701-1-9

Cover Design and Formatting by ebooklaunch.com

36 DAYS

Adam Nelson poured himself a second cup of coffee, sat down at the dinner table in his kitchen, adjusted his tie, and prepared to enjoy his absolute favorite time of the day. It was around 8:15 in the morning. Silence reigned.

Claire had left for work a full hour earlier, and their ten-year-old son Cory had just closed the door heading to his bus stop. Adam loved every minute spent with his loved ones, but sometimes their problems and emotions were a little overwhelming.

The quiet following the usual morning chaos made him feel like he was on top of the world. From 8:15 to 8:30am every weekday morning, Adam found he could just sit in complete stillness and really enjoy his second cup of coffee before he was forced to drive away. The Nelsons lived on the outskirts of New York, and just as this quiet time was the high point of Adam's day, fighting traffic to and from work were the low points. Adam put the commute out of his mind and took a sip of his coffee. He turned his thoughts to the morning's parenting challenges.

Cory did not want to go to school today because of Jeff. Jeff Hammond was the local bully, living just down the street from the Nelsons, and had allegedly pushed Cory out of his place in line for recess in front of the whole class. Adam had his share of bullying experiences when he was growing up, yet, curiously, he had no idea what sort of advice to give his son. Being bullied didn't necessarily build character, but perhaps it was a kind of rite of passage for every young boy. There will always be bullies at every age, and everyone needs to learn how to deal with them sooner or later.

Claire, on the other hand, wanted to accompany Cory to his school with a baseball bat. As amusing as that might be, Adam sometimes didn't think Claire's parenting style was very healthy. The description "control freak" didn't do Claire justice.

Adam picked up his iPad and opened the New York Times app, navigating straight to The Strange section. A recent rash of bizarre stories from around the globe had prompted the paper to begin grouping them all into one section for easy reference. Their biggest problem seemed to be what to name it. They had started with "News of the Strange," switched to "Strange Update," and then finally stuck with "The Strange." Adam saw interest in The Strange articles was outpacing Politics and Sports, and wondered when they would bump it up on the splash screen. CNN was already launching a daily evening show called, "The Phenomenon."

Adam didn't quite know what to make of all the weirdness. The nut carrying the sign outside his office building clearly believed the world was ending, his neighbor Eric thought it was all a mass media conspiracy designed to make people fearful and obedient, but most folks felt just like Adam did: curious, fascinated, and maybe just a little frightened by it all. At least it wasn't another pandemic.

Conscious of his limited leisure window, Adam quickly scanned through The Strange as he slurped his coffee.

The most common Strange articles were always the ones about superhuman feats at times of great stress. When Adam was a boy, he had heard the urban legend of the mother lifting a car off her trapped child right after an accident. Nowadays, it was unusual for a mother *not* to manhandle a twisted pile of steel to save her child. Adam thought of Claire. He suspected she would first lift the car off Cory and then go flip over the car that hit them.

The most interesting Strange stories were well-known myths and tall tales, but now accompanied by actual people involved with actual photos and videos. Fascinated by dinosaurs as a boy, Adam had made a point to follow the recent Loch Ness Monster stories. The official tally of people "suspected of being attacked" by the monster had risen to three. Really what they meant was, "believed to have been swallowed whole." The best pic of the beast by far was taken a couple days ago. The photo was strangely similar to an old well-known Loch Ness Monster picture, with a shadowy outline of a body and thick neck. The new picture was almost the exact same shot, except it looked like someone had cranked up the resolution. It made the first one look obviously fake, showing the actual ripples of the waves and the texture of the monster's skin. In the age of photoshop, it didn't exactly qualify as proof of a monster's existence, but the rest of the stories and pictures sure were pointing that way. Adam hoped he hadn't lied when he told Cory the other day that monsters weren't real.

Today the headline on The Strange was all about the increasing strength of something called the Placebo effect. Adam quickly lost interest as all the talk of data sets and probabilities just reminded him of work. Adam scrolled through a few other sections looking for anything about monsters before glancing at his watch.

It was nearing 8:30. He needed to be at his desk before 9:00, so he gulped the chalky remains of his coffee and headed for the door. Adam was close to becoming manager of the accounting department and was pretty much just waiting for the company to find an excuse to remove his current manager, Melvin. Until then, he needed to keep his punctuality record intact.

Adam worked for a computer hardware company called NextSys. Others might describe accounting at NextSys as stifling, but to Adam, the slow pace allowed him to really connect with his coworkers, whom he genuinely enjoyed. Frank could always be counted on for the mindless morning conversation, which was traditionally scheduled precisely between 10 and 10:30 a.m. after Frank got his first cup of coffee. Not as reliable as Frank, but also fairly consistent was Ellen, the secretary, who would often find an excuse to stop by his desk. Her self-conscious manner always made Adam smile, but Adam was married, and even if he wasn't, Ellen was not his type. Even Melvin, Adam's lousy manager, was amusing to Adam in his own flustered little way. Probably the greatest source of stress at the office for Adam was the fact that he couldn't become manager until his friend Melvin left.

Adam closed and locked the door to his house, mentally preparing himself for the confrontation with Tuesday morning traffic. The thought on everyone's mind was when, where, and how this strange phenomenon might manifest in their own lives. Adam felt secure as he queued into the onramp line for the freeway that if there were to be any unexplained occurrences in his life, there was no way in hell they were going to happen at NextSys.

34 DAYS

Thomas Bonner sat on his porch on a lazy Sunday afternoon and lit a cigar. He stared across the field at the open shed where he had spent his morning. There sat his John Deere 5500, which he affectionately referred to as JD. It had pitifully sat in the same spot since he had parked it there late last September. The stupid thing would not start, and Tom was losing his patience with it. It was not a fuel line problem, not an oil problem, and definitely not a spark plug problem. The engine turned over without a hitch, but never got more than a few revs before dying.

Tom picked up the newspaper and decided he had had enough for the day. It was late March, and he had at least another week or two before the thing needed to be up and running. He would sleep on it and try again in the morning. It would be a cold day in Hell before he took it to Henry's Garage in town, though. The young, smug mechanics at that place always irritated Tom, and he knew damn well they were not the sort of honest mechanics you want around when you live two hundred miles from the nearest major city.

For some time now, Tom had thought every new planting season would be his last. Now in his early sixties, Tom felt he was getting too old for all this fuss. His small, forty-acre beet farm had done well over the years, he had invested cautiously, and so he didn't really need the money anymore. Truthfully, he just didn't know what he would spend his time doing if he wasn't out plowing the fields. Every winter, all he could think about was getting back out and getting to work again. The prospect of sitting on his butt, watching his crops not grow, was more than he could bear. Tom's wife Judy, content with her housekeeping duties, was indifferent to his plight. Even now, he could hear her humming as she worked in the kitchen.

Thomas Bonner puffed on his cigar a few times, took one last look at the tractor and then turned his attention to the local paper. Tom had never paid much attention to the paper. He generally didn't see the sense in worrying about other people's problems when there were always plenty to worry about right here at home. Lately, though, the paper had become much more fascinating.

Something strange was going on in the world, and that was pretty much the beginning and the end of what was common knowledge. Tom was glad Carlos had alerted him about the paper.

Carlos the Mexican, as he was commonly referred to, had a field just a few miles down the road from Tom. Greenfield was a small farming town in central Illinois, and being the only Mexican in Greenfield didn't make Carlos very popular. However, Tom always enjoyed spending time with him, partly due to the fact that being friends with Carlos secretly made Tom feel quite cosmopolitan.

A week ago, Carlos had stopped by and they had shared a beer out on the porch. It was cold that night, and he'd left after just one beer, but Carlos had brought with him a paper, and pointed out a few of the strange articles.

They were grouped in a new section of the paper, called the "Funny Page." The weird articles were always written in an amusingly delicate way. The strangeness of their subject matter was one thing, but Carlos and Tom chuckled at how the journalists would struggle to find wording that didn't make them sound like crazy people, as if their stories somehow had logical explanations. Logical or not, Tom had phoned in a subscription the next day.

One of the articles Carlos had showed Tom that day was about a sighting of The Swamp Thing in Louisiana. It had reportedly lurched across a freeway one evening, causing a four-car pileup. All witnesses described the exact same thing, which was a green, slimy, shuffling humanoid figure. The police had followed the trail of slime into the woods, where, naturally, it disappeared into a swamp. Because of all the weirdness going on, the author of the article did not really know whether it was in fact The Swamp Thing or not, so they couldn't say "a person dressed up like." Then again, what self-respecting journalist would report that "The Swamp Thing" was running around causing highway accidents, so the author had to write convoluted things like "the figure who had caused the incident was reported to have the appearance of a fictional monster, allegedly similar to a creature in a 1950's horror movie." Everyone knew it was The Swamp Thing, but nobody could really admit to the absurdity of a Swamp Thing sighting.

Every day the newspaper seemed to have even more tall tales in it, and today the Funny Page had become the Funny Pages. Tom puffed his cigar and found an article about the studies of telekinesis going on at universities across the country. The article said some people could do it, but they could never seem to do it all the time. Just when whatever official came to verify the result, the telekinetic seemed to get stage fright and was unable to perform. Bizarre. Tom was glad there weren't any universities near Greenfield.

"Dinner!" called Judy from inside the house. Tom wrapped up his paper, put out the cigar, and headed inside.

"Something smells just lovely," said Tom. Tom knew exactly what it was. It was Judy's beef potato stew. He had been married to Judy for twenty-three years, and after that long with someone, he could tell by smelling it if she had put too much cayenne in it. Today it smelled absolutely perfect.

Judy smiled at Tom. She knew Tom knew what was for dinner. She tasted the stew. It tasted perfect. Absolutely perfect.

Judy Bonner had been married to Tom for close to thirty years now, having gotten together after they both escaped disastrous relationships in their early thirties. Shadows of her past always tended to make Judy genuinely grateful for and loving of the present.

Judy prepared the potato stew and set the modest kitchen table, all while still humming and thinking of what she might cook next. Judy accepted responsibility for doing the cleaning, but cooking was her real passion. She thought about making a variant on her classic hotdish tomorrow, unsure whether she should take a break to get rid of some leftovers in the fridge.

Judy placed the stew in the center of the table while Tom washed up in the bathroom. She grabbed her spoon and tasted it one last time, just to be sure she wasn't missing anything. Still perfect.

Lately, all her dinners seemed to be spot-on. She had always felt she was the best chef in town, so truthfully, Judy wasn't really that surprised by her recent successes. She *did* find it a little un-usual that any and all kitchen mishaps (rare as they may have been) had pretty much ceased a few weeks ago. Judy assumed she was just on a roll.

33 DAYS

"You awake?" said Fred.

Keith Pennison dreamily turned away from his computer screen towards his boss, Fred, who was standing at the entrance to his cubicle. Keith tried to remember what it was that he was supposed to be doing.

"Did you get that thing I sent you?" was Fred's question.

Keith found it difficult to concentrate but managed to claw a response out from the dim fog of his mind.

"Yeah, yeah, the performance analytics thing from QA, yeah I got it. I'll take a look at it later."

Keith's response appeared to satisfy Fred, who turned away with a disgruntled, "thanks." Keith wondered if Fred was just trying to see if he was actually working.

Keith turned back to his monitor that displayed a large pile of unread emails, that he had barely touched since he arrived a few hours ago. No, he was not going to look at that crap later. In fact, he was never going to look at that crap. In fact, he was done with all this crap.

Keith was 27 now, having worked at 3D Phonic in Seattle for just over five years. It was Monday, and Keith had spent the morning struggling to care about this job. This was obviously an important moment in human history and wasting any part of it staring at a computer screen just felt absurd.

Keith stood up and took one last look at his cubicle, trying to decide whether any of the trinkets were worth taking with him. He decided he should probably say something.

"Well, I'm leaving now, and I won't be coming back," Keith stated to nobody in particular, but loud enough for people in adjoining cubes to hear him.

Keith had never done anything so dramatic in his life. His heart raced from making such a public spectacle of himself as he walked down the line of cubes towards the door.

Fred was busy hounding someone else for something and noticed him walk by.

"Keith?" asked Fred.

"Bye, Fred," was Keith's response as he kept walking. At this point, Keith was starting to feel good about his decision. As much as he sometimes enjoyed his career in software, there was simply more important things to be doing with his time right now. He had a little money saved up, but he suspected money was going to lose its value soon anyway.

Keith hopped on the bus and rode it to his favorite hole-in-the wall coffee shop, cleverly named The Drip. Seattle was literally overrun with coffee shops, and everyone seemed to have their own favorite establishment where they could feed their caffeine addiction. The Drip was Keith's. It was only a few blocks from his cozy downtown one-bedroom apartment, and the customers could always be counted on to be interesting. With its kitschy wall art and pierced baristas, The Drip was quite hip, bordering on comically hip.

Keith grabbed his usual piping hot mocha, grabbed his favorite seat next to the window, and slyly eyed the eccentric crowd. He tried to calm his nerves, but also couldn't help but smirk. Keith got a text from one of his coworkers and had to assure her that he was not intent on throwing himself off a bridge.

Keith sipped his drink and mused about his place in the grand scheme of things as the coffee orders kept coming. The Drip was buzzing.

Keith knew that the things he could do were not unique, but he also knew the powers he had discovered within himself were not abilities shared by the general public. However, Keith really had no good measure of exactly how unusual his gift was.

Watching the news had made Keith sure he wasn't the only one who found themselves with abilities they could not explain. But the big question was, how many other people out there were hiding it like he was?

"Medium mocha with whip!" called the barista.

A short, skinny, pasty white girl with a nose ring and a red streak in her long, black hair slinked her way to the shelf and furtively snatched the beverage.

Keith thought for a second about the girl and the possibility of her hiding her own secret powers. Would the average person show all their friends, make a YouTube video and then go hunting for their ex? Keith figured it was a pretty safe bet that he was very special. Otherwise, he would be surrounded by more chaos.

It had been almost two weeks since Keith had stumbled upon his special ability while sitting in his bathtub. The occasional bath relaxed him and let his mind wind down after hardcore days at the office. Up until an hour ago, he had been one of four lead developers at 3D-Phonic, and occasionally the job demanded many back-to-back hours of intense caffeine-fueled programming. By the time he arrived home, a decadent soak was the perfect prescription for washing away the maddening logic of the code.

Keith sipped his mocha again and mused about that fateful night.

He had been sitting in the tub staring vacantly at the water as the stillness permeated his small one-bedroom apartment, when he began getting the sensation that he was touching the water with something other than his body. The more he thought about it, the more he was sure that he was sensing the warm, wet essence of the water itself. Suddenly the doorbell rang, and the surface of the water where he was staring vibrated with an electrical intensity. He had almost killed himself leaping out of the bathtub in a watery panic. However, once he regained his composure and realized nothing deadly had fallen into the tub, he returned his attention to the water and discovered he could push tiny ripples across the surface of the water by thought alone. The rest of the night was spent in the bathroom, and from then on, Keith had been experimenting. Keith wondered what he would have said to the Jehovah's Witnesses who rang his doorbell if he had made it to the door.

"Large iced mocha!" yelled the server, waking Keith out of his daydream.

Keith glanced sideways and reached out with his mind to the iced drink sitting on the bar, carefully touching the condensation on the plastic. As he had been practicing, he focused to ignore the air between him and the cup, allowing only the flood of sensory information about the water to enter his mind. The movement of the drips, the chilled temperature of the water, and the slow, melting movement of the ice inside the plastic cup flooded his mind, making him feel like a baby trying to comprehend an elaborate tapestry.

Experimentation had shown that his eyes did not need to be open to use his new talent. Sensing objects felt a lot like someone shining a light directly into his eyeballs, and his reflexive defense was usually to metaphorically "close his eyes" and turn off the ability. Unfortunately, if he kept his eyes closed while feeling around, he was always a bit disoriented when he finished, as he seemed to forget which direction he was facing. There was still much to learn.

A large, round blond girl dressed in black strode up to get her iced mocha. Keith, absorbed in the details of the drink that he could sense, hesitated to break his concentration.

She reached for her drink. Keith gasped as he inadvertently sensed her stomach contents, her skin (both sides), her soiled clothes, and every conceivable detail of the woman's innards between him and her beverage. Repulsed by the instant and horrifically complete knowledge of the woman's intestines, Keith clamped his power shut with an audible, "ugh."

The large woman whirled on Keith with her cold drink in hand.

"What's your problem, asshole?" she demanded.

"Sorry, I mean, I… It wasn't you…" Keith stammered, eyes roaming about the room, unable to look the girl in the face without recalling the contents of her guts.

She turned and stormed away, grumbling something about mental illness.

Keith grabbed his half-empty mocha, donned his jacket, and prepared to leave. No doubt the girl was busy discussing his odd behavior with her friends. Drawing attention to himself was something he was constantly trying to avoid. After checking his phone for the bus times, he headed out the door, trying to forget how a jiggling, convulsing collection of bacteria somehow constituted a human.

20 DAYS

Cory Nelson reluctantly stepped outside his suburban home after calling out the obligatory "bye" to his Dad and headed towards the bus stop. Adjusting his bag, Cory walked determinedly down the sidewalk, all the while trying to quell the rising tide of fear in his stomach. The thought of the impending encounter with Jeff Hammond, a.k.a. "the bully," had been on Cory's mind since he'd woken up. Somehow the stupid jerk always managed to meet up with him before he arrived at their mutual bus stop. At this point, Cory was sure Jeff was waiting by the window until he walked by and then ran out to catch him. Considering the half-a-mile distance to the stop, Jeff's perfect timing went way beyond coincidence.

Cory cautiously neared Jeff's mailbox. No sign of Assface yet.

Looking straight ahead, as nonchalantly as he could, Cory hastened past Jeff's house.

Jeff Hammond burst out of his door pulling his jacket on and hollering, "Fine! Bye, Ma!" over his shoulder with an irritated look on his face as indistinct yelling came from somewhere inside the house.

Jeff Hammond was a pudgy boy. Maybe not fat, exactly, but definitely "husky." That, along with the fact that he was about a foot taller than most boys in his class, sort of made him the bully by default. His size alone was enough to elicit fear among his peers, and his grumpy disposition only confirmed his appointment as the class ogre. Cory wasn't exactly sure if Jeff had any friends, but he knew he wasn't one of them.

Jeff finally seemed to notice Cory and stopped his charge short. He gawked like he hadn't expected to see Cory outside his house, but this was just part of the act. It was too perfect; it was always too perfect. Even though they were catching the same bus, there was no way Jeff just happened to come out of his house at the exact second Cory was in front of it, day after day, every single day. Cory tried starting his walk at different times, sometimes a half hour before the bus came and sometimes cutting it down to the second. Each day, without fail, there was Jeff. It was an ambush; no other explanation was possible.

Cory set his jaw and resumed his walk, sure of the taunts and jeers to follow.

"Hey Squeaker, wait up!" Jeff said. Cory thought there was a new tone in Jeff's voice. It was as if Jeff had lost the meaning behind the abuse, causing the usual bite in "Squeaker" to seem almost cordial.

Labeling Cory "Squeaker" was Jeff's latest game. The worst part about it was that other people were beginning to pick up on it and join in the torment. Kids Cory didn't even know at school had started calling him Squeaker and he feared the name was destined to be engraved on his tombstone. Cory really had no idea how to make it all stop, especially since any time he tried to protest this nickname, his arguments were inevitably compared to the squeaking of an irate mouse.

Cory turned and hotly confronted Jeff, who was still stopped in his driveway like a numbskull.

"Stop calling me Squeaker!" Cory shouted, angered not only by Jeff, but also by his own inability to come up with a sharper retort. He hurried away, hoping to put some distance between himself and the jerk.

"Sure thing, Squeaks," Jeff casually remarked as he resumed his own walk to the bus.

Normally, Jeff would catch up to Cory and begin assaulting him with pokes, taunts, pushes, spit wads, or any number of other barely creative torments. Cory was safe once he reached the bus stop, since there were usually bigger kids there who were groggy and had little tolerance for Jeff's shenanigans. Sometimes Cory tried to outrun Jeff, but running seemed to really anger the brute. If Jeff caught him, he was much less gentle.

However, today was different. Jeff apparently had something on his mind, and kept his distance from Cory, all the way to the bus stop. Cory was relieved by this change of pace, but something about Jeff's actions was bothersome. He glanced back to check on what Jeff was plotting, and found Jeff staring at him, as if he were trying to figure something out. Cory was thankful enough for the reprieve to not ask what was on Jeff's mind. He was probably thinking about something awful like whether Cory would fit into a gym locker.

A few minutes later Cory and the rest of the kids boarded the bus to school without incident. Cory was again relieved that Jeff didn't repeat his favorite nickname in front of anyone else, and again decided he didn't care why.

Cory sat down on his seat, positioned his body and his backpack to ensure nobody sat next to him, and assumed his standard morning slouch, staring vacantly out the window.

As the bus continued its route and filled with kids, the noise level approached its usual dull roar. But just like the last few days, it seemed quieter than usual to Cory. Some key noisemakers were absent.

As the bus approached the school, Cory lifted his head up and looked around the bus for Darren and Suzie. Darren's sarcasm and Suzie's constant jabbering were two voices he knew were missing.

Darren wasn't on the bus, but he thought he remembered something about him going on a camping trip.

Suzie was on the bus, but she was silent, staring out the window like one of the shy kids. Cory wondered what was going on with her. Then his eye caught Jeff, who was also uncharacteristically staring quietly out the window, apparently lost in thought as well. Now that was very strange indeed.

18 DAYS

Thomas Bonner reluctantly drove his pickup truck into the parking lot of Henry's Auto Repair, his shameful excuse for a tractor in tow. To Tom, it defied physics that the thing wouldn't start, but he knew it was time to swallow his pride and let the professional jackasses tell him exactly what it was he was missing. Tom had checked everything he could think to check, and still the stupid tractor acted as if combustion was a foreign concept.

As his truck chugged to a halt, he saw Greg, a husky mechanic in his late 20s, wipe his hands with a dirty cloth and walk out to greet him. Tom braced himself for the inevitable smug greeting, knowing that regardless of what Greg said, Tom would hear, "Hello, why are you stupid today?"

"Howdy," smiled Greg, without any detectable hint of condescension. "Tom, right? Whatcha got there?" he said, sizing up the tractor behind Tom.

Tom gritted his teeth and stepped towards Greg. "Hey there, Greg. I was wondering if you had time to take a look at this old piece of junk. Planting time is almost here, and this bitch of a tractor just will not start."

A strange look passed over Greg's round face, but he quickly set to eyeballing JD.

"Did you check all the usual suspects?" asked Greg as he walked around JD with Tom in tow.

"Sure did. Must'a missed something, cause she turns over once or twice but that's about it," replied Tom.

"Sparkplugs?" asked Greg.

"Nope, double checked each one," Tom said, happy to be shifting the mystery onto someone else's shoulders.

"Gaskets?"

"Nope."

"Fuel lines? Intake valves?"

"Nope, nope."

Greg paused as he rubbed his stubble, staring at his lot of cars, which looked quite a bit fuller than the last time Tom was here.

"It just won't start," Tom offered, starting to feel smug himself, now that the youngster was also finding it to be a puzzle. Greg sighed.

"Alright Tom, I can look at it tomorrow, but I can't say it's at the top of my list. I've got a few other mysteries on my hands." Greg paused and looked at Tom, looking younger and more lost than ever. "It's not been a good week." Greg was no longer smiling. "When did ya need it by?" he asked.

"End of the week is fine," answered Tom, knowing full well he would be lucky to get it back in two weeks. Tom went to go unhitch JD, now surer than ever that Greg didn't know what the hell he was doing.

18 DAYS

Keith swiped his key fob to the front door of his apartment building and the door buzzed obediently. A few more steps put him in front of the grid of lock boxes for mail, and Keith looked around to make sure nobody was watching. The little security camera was pointed at the door, and he was able to see both entrances from where he stood.

It had been close to two weeks since he dramatically ended his software engineering career, and in that time, Keith had been experimenting. Opening his mailbox with his mind was next on his list.

Keith reached out with his mind just as he had done before and felt the coldness of the steel and brass that made up the locking mechanism for his mailbox. Unexpectedly, Keith had been finding that the less he focused on what he was doing with his mind, the easier the tasks seemed to be.

Keith ignored the sensory input as much as possible and just willed the lock to turn. The little door popped open with a squeak, just as if Keith had used his key.

Keith wondered if a door he was unfamiliar with would be as easy. He looked at his neighbor's box and it popped open immediately, just the same as his, with nothing but a stray thought's worth of effort.

Keith had another thought and took a step back. All 28 remaining boxes popped open and swung out in unison, accompanied by a chorus of hinge whines.

Keith quickly slammed all the boxes shut, afraid someone was going to come around the corner and think he was robbing the place. There was something different going on here. He hadn't been aware of touching each box individually, but somehow something got translated so that he moved all of them at the same time.

Keith realized he hadn't re-locked the boxes after he shut them. He figured he should be able to do it all at once like he had opened them, but he didn't know exactly how he had done that.

Someone walked by outside talking on their phone and Keith decided he had just better fix it as fast as possible. He went down the line clicking each lock back into place, one after the other.

Flustered, Keith turned to head up the stairs and then paused. Out of sheer habit, he pulled out his key, opened his box normally, and snatched his few scraps of junk mail. Following his normal routine calmed his nerves and made him feel camouflaged like a normal person once again.

Keith started walking up the three flights of dingy stairs to his apartment. Arriving at his door, he held out his hand as if he was pushing it open, yet actually used his mind to shove the heavy metal door open. The effort of this daily test always confirmed one thing: his power was getting stronger.

14 DAYS

The light turned green and Adam Nelson pulled onto the 280 freeway with the pedal of his silver SUV pushed to the floor. It was the same entrance he had taken every workday since he moved into his current home six years ago, using the same SUV he had bought two years ago, yet this time Adam felt like something was different.

In the last few days, Adam had come to realize he was growing increasingly afraid of this very moment. He dreaded getting on the highway, and he had no idea why.

Adam tried to ignore the nagging feeling, switched on his turn signal, and watched the oncoming traffic in the freeway entrance lane. Nothing was different, nothing was weird, he reassured himself. He was just being paranoid.

Adam accelerated his SUV onto the freeway and merged two lanes to the left, just as he always did. In his usual spot, one lane to the right of the fast lane, Adam tried to calm himself. He watched the cars around him as he did every day, kept his usual distance, and told himself that there was nothing wrong.

But something *was* wrong. He simply could not deny the fact that when he looked out at the dozen or so vehicles in his view, something looked off about them. Every car was hurtling along beside him with its own tiny little individual movements, in line with the slightest touches of the wheels of the drivers. It was those little movements that were driving him crazy. There was something more to them, something unnatural in the wiggles of the traffic around him.

Adam kept his usual safe distance from the bumper in front of him and tried his hardest to locate the source of these feelings. It made no sense why he felt uneasy doing what should be a completely normal part of his daily routine.

Adam focused his attention on the driver in front of him, which happened to be a little red Prius. It must have rather touchy steering, because Adam noticed every little movement of the wheel. The car would cruise in a straight line, veer slightly to the right, and when it got close to the dotted white line, the driver would pull it a little to the left. Adam thought of the Prius driver, who most likely was a young professional, probably had tea this morning, and was also probably feeling a little nervous about this drive.

Adam noticed he was beginning to sweat a little and decided on a different approach. He decided to think of the drive as a video game, and concentrated not on the other drivers, but only on the location of his car, the dotted lines, and the velocities of the cars around him.

This new tactic seemed to help as Adam felt his fear slowly recede. Only when a car came particularly close to him, or when someone was merging next to him, did he again feel the dread.

Claire Nelson merged onto the 280 with ease as the overhead-cam engine on her Ford Mustang roared with authority. As she did, the two cars on the freeway closest to her reacted bizarrely. The car to her left swerved wide in anticipation of her overshooting her lane, and the car behind her braked heavily to give her an unusually large amount of leeway. In the last few days, Claire had noticed other drivers seemed more skittish than usual. She wasn't sure if everybody decided to have an extra cup of coffee in the morning or if all just agreed to start jumping at ghosts.

Claire vaguely remembered a feature on CNN about this very phenomenon. For some unknown reason, some people were losing their nerve on the freeways. Claire was not one of these people, though. That was for damn sure.

Claire flipped her blinker and quickly claimed her spot in the fast lane. Every day, the ride to work became even more entertaining than the day before. She didn't know what it was, but she liked it. Claire felt more in control, and surprisingly more aware of all the drivers around her.

Claire merged in front of a shiny new BMW convertible and accelerated. She was not just unfazed by the maneuver—she felt energized by it. Oddly, the BMW did not react to her at all.

Claire decided to ease down on the aggressive driving a bit. Her husband Adam hated it when she drove this way, and anyway, there was something weird happening on the freeways. Every fiber of her soul assured her that she was not in any danger, but she let the logical part of her mind take control. The fact was, something unusual was happening during the morning commute, the most dangerous part of everyone's lives, and that alone was reason enough to exercise caution.

As relief washed over him, Adam finally reached the off-ramp to Monroe drive, his standard exit on the way to work. As he waited at the stoplight, he took deep breaths and tried to get a grip on exactly what about the freeway was driving him nuts.

He made his left turn and followed a brown Ford Explorer onto the side street. Was it really the freeway traffic that was causing the problem, or was it something else? According to MSNBC, a large portion of commuters were feeling the same things. Logic indicated the strange feelings on the freeway had to be a symptom, not a cause. Hopefully, somebody would figure it out quickly and put an end to it, or at least explain to the world how, exactly, one was supposed to deal with it. And there was no way the exponential increase in unexplained supernatural phenomena in the media in recent weeks was a coincidence. This was not some kind of world-wide hallucination about the morning drive. With all the scientists and physicists in the world, there was simply no excuse for global mysteries to go unsolved like this.

Adam felt his confidence returning as he followed the brown Explorer in front of him down the side street towards his office building. Humanity was going to figure this one out, and probably soon. In retrospect, the answer will probably be so obvious that it will be amazing that we didn't see it all along. Just like Adam knew the brown Explorer was going to turn into his office parking lot, America would see the course ahead and plan accordingly.

As the Explorer slowed and then turned left in front of him, Adam was struck with uncertainty. He did not remember ever seeing the car at work, and he didn't actually know its destination. But he was 100% certain a moment ago that it was going to turn. How could he have known, without a doubt, that he was going to follow the car in front of him in a left-hand turn? Was he psychic, and if so, what did that even mean? Did his psychic powers only apply to non-freeway driven SUVs near his office?

Adam put the unanswerable questions out of his mind as he assumed his usual parking spot, welcoming the familiarity of his office. He must have just seen the Ford at work before and assumed subconsciously that it was headed to the office garage.

Sure.

14 DAYS

It was Sunday, and just like every Sunday morning, Thomas and Judy Bonner were headed to Meadowview Methodist Church.

Growing up in a small farming community, going to church wasn't entirely optional. It had been a part of both Tom and Judy's lives for as long as they could remember, but not so much for the spiritual aspect as for the social. When the closest family was often a twenty-minute drive away, most people looked forward to the weekly Sunday gathering, a time when adults were expected to be cordial and kids were expected to be quiet.

Tom never really considered himself to be a spiritual man, but he did like to be agreeable. For most of his early life, Tom had doubted such things as a heavenly father or pearly gates. However, he never admitted these feelings to anyone, as that sort of anti-social talk didn't really have a place in Greenfield.

Tom folded the last loops of his tie as he walked out the door to where Judy was patiently waiting behind the wheel of their idling truck. Judy despised being late to anything, and Tom could tell the 10 a.m. start time was always on her mind, even though they never failed to arrive less than half an hour before services started. Tom climbed in and slammed the door behind him with one hand as his tie continued to frustrate his other hand. Judy backed up and started driving.

The ride to church was a quiet one. Both Tom and Judy were anxious to hear what the good reverend was planning to say about the state of the world. Normally, apocalyptical events supported Christian theology, but there was definitely nothing in the Bible that said Bigfoot would walk the earth again.

Reverend Bailey was a good man, Tom mused as Judy turned them onto the paved road and picked up speed. Approximately three years ago, the town's former head holy man, Reverend Foster, had suffered a stroke, and Bailey had been forced to take over. Bailey was not even thirty years old yet, and compared to the soothing wisdom of Foster, whom Tom had known since childhood, Bailey's drippy, predictable sermons often left a bad taste in Tom's mouth. At least he was trying, that much was apparent. Bailey did indeed have a lot of heart, but the time during which the reverend was lecturing was always the low point of trip, in Tom's opinion.

Not everyone held Tom's opinion of the reverend. In fact, it often seemed that a citizen's age was directly related to whether Reverend Bailey was a vibrant breath of fresh air or a sorry replacement for a wise old man.

They arrived at church and took their usual seats. Judy made her rounds, catching up on gossip, while Tom said hi to Edgar and Carlos. Edgar, like many attendees, seemed a little on edge.

Tom's personal feelings on The Lord had grown somewhat late in his life. When Judy had taken ill a few years back with a dangerous-but-not-always-fatal form of breast cancer, Tom had placed his faith in God and prayed his pants off. His prayers appeared to have paid off with Judy's full recovery. Even though Judy had better-than-even odds, Tom had felt his faith renewed by the entire experience.

Bailey finally took the podium and started the service. It quickly became clear that the reverend had no more answers than anyone else as to what was causing all the strangeness across the land. In fact, he appeared even more bothered than most, probably because everyone was looking to him for answers. Inaudible disappointment flickered through the crowd. At one point, Bailey addressed the strangeness directly.

"Although I may not have insight into the oddness of these times, I do have one piece of advice that I guarantee will see you through. Hold onto your faith, my friends. It does not matter what the future brings as long as we maintain our faith in God. Through Him, faith will see us through even the darkest of times. Whatever happens, we will come through it, together, with faith."

Disappointing as this was, it was not unexpected. Nobody really thought Bailey would say anything new. Even so, and even though Bailey's lack of experience was obvious, Tom still felt comforted by the pastor's words. Putting faith in the Lord was always relaxing to Tom. Aside from the usual reassurance that everything will be all right in the end, there was always something elusive about faith that felt very much like truth to Tom.

After the services, as Tom and Judy had said their byes and were walking away from the church, Edgar approached them.

Tom had known Edgar for close to ten years, which, for the size of town they lived in, was not really all that spectacular. They had never gone to school together, nor did Tom ever spend much time with Edgar. Living alone on his farm, Edgar had developed certain anti-social tendencies that tended to keep him living alone on his farm. The most offensive of which was the fact that Edgar didn't seem to have any awareness of his own body odor or his breath.

However, Edgar's land was only five or so miles past Tom's, and regardless of their neighborly proximity, Tom had always tried not to let bodily odors interfere with friendships, so he and Edgar were on good terms.

Edgar shambled up to Tom and Judy, who turned towards him when they noticed his approach. Tom braced himself for the smell.

"Uh, hey there Tom…Ma'am," Edgar half-nodded to Judy as he closed in on Tom. Relieved that she was not needed in Edgar's discussion, Judy nodded and smiled warmly at Edgar as she continued her walk to their truck.

"Howdy Edgar. How's things with you?" Tom hoped it would be quick, though Edgar's unease was palpable.

"Hey, uh, have you heard anything, uh, weird, uh lately?"

Tom's blank face was only disturbed the wrinkle of his nose. Tom wondered exactly which weird item in the newspaper Edgar might be referring to.

"You know, uh, at night?" Edgar continued. He searched Tom's face for some hint of recognition. "The wolves?"

Tom sucked his breath. Edgar wasn't talking about the news.

"Edgar, what in Sam hell are you talking about?" Tom asked incredulously. Weirdness in the paper was fine, but Tom didn't like the idea of something that might be dangerous so close to his home. "There haven't been wolves in these parts in over fifty years! Hell, probably a hundred!"

Edgar was flustered. "Well, maybe dey ain't wolves, mebbie sled dogs or something? You know, mebbie someone's got some huskies? I mean, ya ain't heard em then?"

A sled dog team in central Illinois was almost as ridiculous as a wolf pack.

"Well, what are you trying to say, Edgar? Howling? You hearing dogs?"

"If ya ain't heard them, then ya already gave me mah answer, didn't ya?" Edgar was obviously hurt by Tom's skepticism. "Take care Tom."

"Wait, Edgar, hang on, I was just asking," called Tom, but Edgar had already stormed off. Tom watched Edgar go, debating whether to follow, before finally deciding to spare Edgar any more embarrassment.

Any other day, Tom wouldn't have given Edgar's nervous ramblings a second thought, but the memory of the morning newspaper was still fresh in his mind. Wolves in Illinois was not nearly as preposterous as it should be.

As Judy watched him get into the passenger side of his truck, Tom paused again. It occurred to him that Edgar probably didn't read the paper. In fact, Tom wasn't sure Edgar could read. Tom's pungent neighbor might not be aware of the strange happenings elsewhere in the world.

"Everything all right with Edgar?" asked Judy. "He looked a little off."

"He's fine." Tom shut the door. "Thinks he hears wolves."

"Wolves?" Judy said dubiously, echoing Tom's sentiment. Then she remembered the Funny Page, and her frightened eyes met Tom's.

Tom turned and looked out the window. "Yeah, strange, huh?"

Neither spoke on the ride home.

10 Days

The elevator chimed its arrival on the sixth floor of the Clark Centre building. Claire Nelson strode from the elevator towards the offices of S-Mobile, sipping on her morning cappuccino.

People had problems. This was the usual mantra of Claire's job, but lately it had been taking on a whole new meaning. Managing eleven entry-level phone support representatives at a cellular phone company was no easy task, but Claire was well suited for the job. Not only did her commanding personality make her a natural leader, but she was also extremely adept at dealing with angry customers who got too rowdy for her more sensitive employees.

Normally the people who had the problems were the ones on the other end of the phone line. Often Claire's cubicle precinct was a madhouse of courteous efforts to placate irate cell phone customers, something that Claire found not entirely unpleasant. Lately, however, the problems were coming from her employees, and these were not the kind of problems Claire enjoyed dealing with.

Claire tossed her empty paper cup in the trash and began logging into her computer while simultaneously playing her voice mails. Before she could turn her attention to her computer, Gertrude, the portly office gossip queen, burst into Claire's office with much fanfare. Gertrude wore her hair in a blond bun on the top of her head, and always seemed to be wearing too much makeup. Claire smiled politely as Gertrude eagerly embarked on her morning tirade.

"Morning hon! Sorry, no time to chat, Lloyd's got some sort of inferiority complex that is making him, and well quite frankly us too, all kinds of wound-up crazy. I am serious, Claire, you have got to get over there. He is absolutely useless on the phone and poor Carl can't seem to get his act together next to Lloyd's meltdown—but then again who can blame him—I'm three rows down and I can barely stand to hear it!" Gertrude paused long enough to suck in a lung full of air, "Meanwhile, Cheryl has some—"

Claire sometimes wished Gertrude would give it a rest, especially first thing in the morning. She had learned, though, that it was best to let Gertrude do her thing, and be the big, jiggly information sponge that she liked to be. Obnoxious or not, people like Gertrude were useful to managers.

"—sort of crippling driving problem, the poor thing came in all wet, looking like a drowned rat! When I went to go check on her, I realized it was all just sweat from her drive! Good Lord, I've never seen such a thing! Sweat! Looked like she ran a marathon! I haven't heard her on the phone yet, but—" Gertrude had plopped down on a chair in the office, but Claire was already heading out the door to address the Lloyd situation. Gertrude raised her voice to be sure Claire heard her.

"—if you want my opinion, hah, and everyone does, right?" Gertrude took another breath. "If you want my opinion, the little thing just needs a Zanax!" she yelled as the office door closed behind Claire.

Claire strode over to where Lloyd was allegedly melting and upsetting the rest of her otherwise-chipper employees.

Lloyd Moore wasn't exactly the guy nobody liked; he was more like the guy nobody loved. He was a decent performer, didn't say much, kept to himself. Talking to him generally gave one the feeling that he wasn't the most social cat in the room, but Claire felt this trait probably helped him in dealing with irate customers, as it is usually harder to yell at someone that you feel sorry for.

Claire assessed the situation as she approached her line of cubicles. Lloyd was staring at his computer with his head in his hands, his straight brown hair tussled and hanging limp over his head. He stared at the computer screen with a blank, almost forlorn look. He looked like he had failed miserably in some great endeavor. Lloyd's earpiece was still in, so Claire assumed he had just gotten off a rough call. It was rare, but occasionally a customer could be so ruthless and personal that even veteran employees can get rattled. Lloyd wasn't quite a rock, but he had also been around a few years, so this kind of a meltdown was fairly unexpected.

As she neared the disaster site, Claire confirmed Lloyd's phone light was off and then glanced at his cubicle neighbors. To Lloyd's right was Carl, a bald, middle-aged man with a mustache who was looking very irritated as he tried to concentrate on his work. Carl had the peculiar trait of turning different shades of red, depending on how frustrated he was. Nobody was on his phone either, but Claire could see Carl had already passed Stage One of crimson.

Lloyd's other cubicle neighbor was probably never going to arrive. Amir had never come back from his week-long vacation and it was safely assumed he had quit without notice. He hadn't been there very long, and Claire wasn't very broken up to see him go. His Indian accent always had customers accusing him of residing in India, which didn't support the company's advertised stance of using American support representatives.

"Hey Lloyd." Claire knew it was probably best if Lloyd offered up his problem on his own rather than asking him about it.

"Hi Claire," was his lifeless response. He didn't turn to face her, which was strange for Lloyd, who was normally eager to please.

"So …" replied Claire, trying to think of how best to put it. "What's up?"

"I can't do it!" burst Lloyd, turning towards Claire and exposing the tear lines on his face. "I can't take any more calls, I can't listen to one more, I just can't … I can't …" Lloyd trailed off.

This kind of negativity had always irritated Claire. When someone tells you that they can't do something, it seemed to her that they were fishing for you to tell them that they can. Claire suppressed her contempt and waited for Lloyd to finish, since he obviously had much more to say.

Lloyd regained some of his composure and started angrily, "I came in this morning, and I just knew I was going to get an awful call. You know me, somehow first thing in the morning, I just always get them."

Claire knew this was not the best moment to disagree, so Lloyd's rant continued.

"So, I pick up the first call, hoping against hope that somehow, today, my morning would go differently, and guess what? I get Mr. Zimmer. Now let me tell you about Mr. Zimmer." Lloyd motioned to his monitor where Mr. Paul Zimmer's information was displayed. "Mr. Zimmer is a lawyer. Mr. Zimmer is not a nice lawyer …" Lloyd trailed off.

Claire spotted her chance for humor and interjected, "Oh, you thought you were going to get the nice lawyer …"

Unamused, Lloyd shot an angry look at Claire.

Claire immediately revised her strategy. "Look, Lloyd, we all get nightmare people on the phone from time to time, that's what this job is. Someone has to talk to the crazies. You know that. You've done that. I've heard you do it. And I've heard you do it well."

Claire checked her progress in Lloyd's face before continuing. Though he had resumed his defeated stare at the monitor, Claire knew that Lloyd was listening, so she went on.

"Now I don't want to hear that you can't handle a little whiny lawyer piss-fest, no matter what time of day it is," Claire started.

"I can't," Lloyd mumbled as he shook his head with an indignant frown.

Having dealt with crumbling-employee crises many times in the past, Claire was well within her element, but the utter Lloyd-ness of this was starting to get to her.

Claire's silence drew Lloyd's eyes up from his monitor. Claire quickly picked back up where she left off.

"I'm sorry, I don't believe you, Lloyd."

It happened suddenly, approaching like an earthquake from a distance.

"You can do this," said Claire quietly, but the last word was like a clap of thunder coming from Lloyd, somehow echoing in Claire's ears even though she had not raised her voice.

Lloyd wide eyes told Claire that he must have heard it too. Or heard something.

They gaped at each other for a moment, trying to understand what had just happened. Carl leaned out from his cubicle to check on the pause in the drama.

Claire realized the rest of the office continued to ring and murmur in the background, unaware of what she and Lloyd may or may not have just heard or felt.

Claire straightened, and out of managerial responsibility, mumbled to Lloyd, "Okay?"

Lloyd blinked, his face searching for his original crisis, and stammered back, "um, uh, yeah…" He quickly turned to his screen, not making eye contact with Claire.

Claire walked back to her office, where Gertrude eagerly awaited the results of the meeting.

Nothing about the current "bizarreness" going on in the world had bothered Claire much up until this point. On the way back to her office, she decided it was time to start paying more attention to the weirdo news that her husband was so captivated with, especially if it was going to affect her ability to manage.

Gertrude was waiting to pounce.

"So what was it? Did Lloyd's dog die? Or did his wife leave him a second time?" Gertrude quipped with mean little smirk.

"No, Gertrude, Lloyd was just having a bad morning, like we all do sometimes." Claire sat down with her eyes focused on her computer but could tell Gertrude wasn't buying it. "Hey, can you close the door when you leave? I need to get some things done."

Gertrude's face went from skeptical to pouty.

"Well, all right, ma'am, I'll leave you be. But I'll be back if there are any more tears!" Gertrude warned as she closed the door.

Claire sifted through the morning stack of emails, trying to push the incident with Lloyd out of her mind. It seemed that Team D, who worked three rows down from Claire's team, was doing spectacularly, blowing away all their numbers. Claire wished her team was more like team D.

Around the same time on the other side of town, Claire's husband, Adam Nelson, stood outside the Nelson's townhome staring at his Ford Explorer. He should be getting in to go to work now, but he wasn't. Adam's skin was crawling, and he couldn't shake the feeling that he should figure out why before he got behind the wheel again.

The story in the Strange Pages this morning was that mass transit traffic had been going through the roof, and that people were developing aversions to driving themselves down the road. Adam never thought he would be one of them. "Freeway Fear," they were calling it. Adam could no longer pretend this feeling of the willies was his imagination. He must have contracted the Freeway Fear. It definitely hadn't happened overnight, in fact he could have sworn it was weeks ago when he first felt there was something weird happening on the way to work. Just yesterday morning, by the time he walked into NextSys, his heart was racing as if he had just delivered a speech to a crowded room.

Adam pushed these thoughts away, got into his Explorer, and started the engine. Everyone was sure the Freeway Fear had something to do with the recent strangeness going on in the world, but nobody seemed to be able to pinpoint exactly where the fear was coming from. Having just read as much as he could about it this morning, Adam reviewed the facts in his head before putting the car in drive.

Driving-related accidents and fatalities had declined sharply, mostly due to considerably less traffic on the road, so Adam was sure the Freeway Fear had to be some sort of shared hysteria, and not really any kind of actual danger.

There were also the unflattering facts the Freeway Fear revealed about Adam's personality. According to the Associated Press, people prone to develop the Freeway Fear were generally more "sensitive," for lack of a better word. People with aggressive personalities like Adam's wife Claire, who did not back down from confrontations, seemed not to notice the Fear. People like Adam, often portrayed on TV as pencil-pushing doormats, were apparently likely to become even more cowardly than they already were.

Adam started his drive with a determination to drive more like Claire. She told him that she didn't notice anything unusual driving to work, so maybe he just needed to be more of an asshole. How could that be hard? Claire's way of driving had always given Adam heart palpitations. As Adam waited in the onramp queue to I-280, he wondered if screaming obscenities at other cars like Claire did would help. He felt like it might.

The onramp light flashed and it was his turn to accelerate. Adam slowly and painfully gained speed, preparing to merge into the fast-flowing rush hour traffic. Immediately, Adam's head filled with a rush of chaotic ideas about which way he should go, how fast he should go, and where he should go. Adam focused and claimed his spot in the furthermost right lane.

After a few minutes of driving, Adam felt in control enough to try to observe where these strange feelings were coming from. The only thing certain was that these feelings were coming from the other drivers. There was simply something very wrong with them.

A man driving an old, rusted pickup truck braked sharply in front of Adam, and Adam cautiously braked after reducing his speed. But then something popped into his mind, that the driver was 77 years old and irritated about his daughter marrying a Latino man. As the feeling faded, Adam felt disgusting inside. There was no reason he should know anything about that person.

When Adam was nearing his office and merged towards the exit, he spotted a woman in a little red Chevy Spark zooming up behind him. Adam glanced in his rearview to see that the Spark was going faster than he expected and needed to brake to let him in. Adam flushed as an overwhelming feeling emitted from the driver of the Spark. It was if the existence of Adam's Explorer was just plain wrong to her, and Adam felt panic that maybe she was right. Adam caught a glance of her face as she braked. She looked pissed.

The whole thing left Adam shuddering as he drove into the company parking lot. Adam had a new number one priority today, which was to sign up for the rapidly growing carpool at work. The newspaper said carpooling was the best cure for the Freeway Fear, and Adam knew it was time to put his pride aside.

The rest of the morning more or less continued as usual for Adam. Nobody noticed the tiny bead of sweat on his brow as he walked in.

Frank arrived at his usual time and eagerly dove into his usual list of complaints. Frank was a short man who loved to talk about how everyone else wasn't doing their jobs correctly. 45 minutes later, Frank was still going strong.

"And so I said to her, 'why don't you just use Excel? Why do you have to make it so complicated?' How can someone be a

CPA for that many years and not know how to write an Excel macro?" jabbered Frank. It seemed to Adam that the length of Frank's little visits seemed to be getting longer every day.

"Uh huh," murmured Adam, pretending to focus on his computer. Adam wondered if it was a symptom of some sort of personal problem, or maybe some kind of work-avoidance tactic, but Frank just seemed to want to keep talking.

"Hell, I was writing macros in high school, and not even in Excel. But when you deal with large piles of data like we do, it just doesn't make sense to not know something so basic. I wonder if Melvin knows this," said Frank, pausing to muse at the ceiling.

Adam said nothing and focused on his computer. Normally Frank would take the hint. But not today.

"It just makes you think, right?" continued Frank. "What sort of skills are they screening for nowadays? Back when I got hired, Excel was just about all they asked about."

Adam decided he had enough.

"Hey Frank, I got a meeting at 10 and need to get ready," said Adam. Normally he would never be so rude with Frank, but he really did have a meeting.

Frank blanched and shot a look at his watch. With wide eyes, he bolted out of Adam's office. Adam shook his head, wondering if Frank had talked himself past a deadline and was missing something important.

Adam got up and headed to his meeting. It was a small meeting, only between Melvin, himself, and Ellen, so Adam figured it probably wouldn't take very long.

Melvin and Ellen were already seated across from each other in the tiny space that was the company's sad excuse for a conference room. They were staring at each other with mildly stunned looks on their faces, and barely seemed to notice Adam's entrance.

"Hey, uh, am I interrupting something?" Adam joked as he took his seat.

Their response was disturbing.

Melvin stammered, "uh, no Adam, you are not," and immediately focused on the task at hand, taking control of the meeting and summarizing the issue.

Melvin's formality, along with Ellen's obvious relief, made Adam think he had, indeed, interrupted something. The thought of anything "personal" between Melvin and Ellen was both morally and physically disgusting to Adam, but the look on their faces stuck with Adam. This "let's-not-talk-about-it" look of mild alarm was something he had seen around the office a lot lately.

The rest of the meeting continued normally, save for the hint of embarrassment between Melvin and Ellen. The subject of the meeting was how to divide up Katelyn's workload. Katelyn was one of their younger employees who, up until a week ago, was also one of their most promising. Katelyn had quit without any prior notice other than a short voice mail on Melvin's machine. Katelyn's quitting had been a blow to the team for a whole slew of reasons: Everybody liked Katelyn, Katelyn seemed to get along with everyone, Katelyn was very responsible, honest, and above all, by all outward appearances, Katelyn loved her job. The biggest reason, however, that Katelyn's leaving was disturbing, was that people were unexpectedly quitting their jobs all over the world.

The events in the Strange Pages were becoming uncomfortably ordinary.

8 Days

Judy Bonner stared indecisively at the bag of groceries that sat on the linoleum kitchen countertop in front of her, trying to decide whether she should be worried about it.

It was a sunny late afternoon in Illinois, and Tom was in his usual spot on the porch, listening to the sounds of the sleepy farm. The constant hum of insects, interspersed with the busy conversations of birds, all created a soothing rhythm periodically punctuated by the puffs of Tom's cigar.

Judy had just returned from the grocery store and was preparing to cook…something. But that was exactly what caused her to hesitate. Usually when she cooked, she decided to make something, planned, bought ingredients, and did her best. Lately, however, it seemed that the less planning she did, and the more spontaneously and carefree she cooked, somehow the better the meal came out.

However, today at the store, Judy thought she might have gone too far. Without any idea of what to make, and with only the idea of wanting to make something fantastic again, Judy had bought two bags worth of ingredients for some fish-based entree that she had never made before.

Judy thought to herself, I'm just making fish. No big deal. She began to get out a mixing bowl and saucepan before pausing. She looked at the saucepan, thinking about the three spices and the oil that needed to go in there. She knew just how each would taste and how much to add, yet she couldn't help wondering how she knew that without even looking at the names of the spices she just bought.

"What!?" hollered Tom from the porch.

"What, hun?" Judy called back over her shoulder, still eyeing her saucepan suspiciously.

"Did you say something?" asked Tom.

"No, not me," answered Judy absent mindedly, as she put the saucepan down and decided to unpack the rest of her mystery ingredients. She was sure she had never tried this kind of fish before either, but if she'd learned anything from the past few weeks, it was that this was going to be tasty.

Tom walked inside with an incredulous look on his face, as Judy turned around, surprised by Tom's interruption of his daily sitting ritual.

"What's the matter, Tom?" she ventured, suddenly concerned by the look on his face.

"Uhh… welp…" stammered Tom. "You see, I was just sittin there, like I do, you know, and, uh…" Judy searched his face for clues.

The phone rang, and Tom jumped with a start.

"Well, settle down there Mr. Bonner, it's just the phone." Judy chuckled as she glided across the room. "What in the world has got you so on edge?" she asked as she picked up the receiver of the old cordless phone. "Bonner residence," she answered cheerfully, still suspiciously eyeing Tom.

The voice on the other end of the line seemed shaky.

"Hey Judy, it's Greg, down at Henry's auto repair?" Greg sounded stressed.

"Well, why hello there Greg!" Judy had met Greg several times around town, and he seemed like a sweet guy.

Tom plopped down on the couch, looking as if he was just punched in the stomach. Judy hoped Greg would be quick so she could figure out what was wrong with Tom.

"Do you want to talk to-," Judy started, assuming the call was tractor-related. But Greg cut her off.

"No, just tell him to come get it," said Greg's in a hurried voice.

"Okay, so it's all ready then? I'll let him-," Judy started but again was interrupted by Greg.

"No, it won't start. I won't fix it. Just come get it," said Greg.

Greg's choice of words was bizarre. Uncomfortable dealing with mechanics, Judy said, "I think you really should be talking to Tom," and began walking over to the couch where Tom was.

As she was about to pass the phone, she heard Greg say one last time, "no, just come get it," and hang up.

Judy looked at the receiver as if it was sprouting tentacles and then placed it back in its charger station.

"What's the word?" asked Tom nervously.

"Well, Tom, that was just about the oddest call I've ever had," stated Judy. "You remember Greg from Henry's Auto Repair?"

Tom swallowed hard and nodded. Something had definitely spooked him.

"Well, he just called to say you have to pick up JD, that they're not going to fix it. I have never in all my years heard a mechanic say such a thing. Usually, they're happy to charge you an arm and a leg for fiddling with your car for weeks; even then they only end up making it worse," Judy looked to Tom for confirmation. Tom just stared back at her, pale faced.

After waiting a second for an explanation without getting one, Judy inquired, "What is it, Tom?"

Tom paused. "There is just something very kooky about all of this." The blank stare on Judy's face meant Tom had to continue. "I told you there was nothing wrong with that goddam machine! Little Greg probably just gave up. It may be Henry's auto, but Greg ain't no Henry, you know what I mean?"

Satisfied with Tom's response, but still unsure about what was spooking her husband, Judy ventured, "Well, now what?" Judy was referring to this year's planting season, something that she knew was on Tom's mind as well.

"Hell, I don't know. We could go buy a new rig, of course. But do we want to dip into our savings when we don't even know how many more seasons we are going to shoot for? Maybe this is the universe saying it is time to throw in the towel." A worried look came over Tom's face again.

"And what was all that before Greg called?" Judy asked. "Why were you acting all funny?"

"Now Judy, this is gonna sound crazy, but hear me out," Tom said.

Judy put her hands on her hips and prepared herself for her husband's craziness.

"Right before he called, when I was out on the porch, minding my own business, out of nowhere all I could think about was Greg and JD not starting," Tom said, looking over at Judy with wide eyes.

"What in the hell? Are you psychic now, Tom?" Judy asked sarcastically as she turned back towards the kitchen.

"I told ya it was crazy!" Tom stood up and grabbed his jacket. "I could always haul JD to Bisby. That would take all day and they'd probably take my money first before telling me the bastard won't start. Whatever, I guess I better go down to Henry's and have a talk with them," sighed Tom.

Judy smiled at Tom's decisiveness. Though she often knew more about what was going on than Tom did, she liked it when he acted with certainty.

"Say hi to Greg if you see him," called Judy over her shoulder as Tom walked out to his truck. Judy returned her attention back to dinner. Still a mystery fish dish. Still going to be excellent. She was sure of it.

7 Days

The Westvale federal penitentiary had never felt so full of promise.

Jacob Christenson laid back on his top bunk, smoked cigarettes, and watched the tiny TV in the corner of his cell with a grin on his face. The entire prison was simmering because of what had happened in D block the other day. The guards had rolled a total lockdown across the entire facility, but that didn't stop the story from spreading like wildfire.

Two days ago, Jacob had been hanging out in the yard with Darrey when the C/Os had unceremoniously herded them into their foul cages. After the unexpected lockdown, it didn't take long for the story to come rushing down the line. And what a story it was.

Mad Jimmy, one of the resident psycho nutballs, had started laughing hysterically while playing cards, and then suddenly crap had started flying around by itself. Or, more accurately, Mad Jimmy made crap fly around. It was easy to figure out Jimmy was in control of the things when you considered what the things did. The wooden table Jimmy was playing cards on had allegedly launched itself at Chris Dietrick's forehead. Dietrick was a big player in D block, though Jacob rarely had any dealings with him. Chris was more of the large, bald, mean type, while Jacob considered himself the smaller, quieter, I-will-slit-your-throat type. It was well known, however, that Mad Jimmy was one of Chris's favorite playthings, and he played frequently.

The wooden table had reportedly done quite a bit of damage to Dietrick's forehead, although these word-of-mouth stories always got implausibly imaginative when it came to gory details. Depending on who you believed, Chris either fell down with a large, bloody bruise, or his head exploded like a grapefruit.

With Dietrick down, Mad Jimmy began causing the rest of the tables and chairs to fly all over the place hitting the guards and other inmates he didn't like. The guards tackled him, but before they could knock him unconscious, guard Herwick took a twenty (or thirty or fifty) foot flight directly into a wall.

Mad Jimmy had not been seen since. The word from the infirmary was that the nurses were keeping him fully sedated until further notice.

As Jacob watched the headline news channel on the little TV in the corner of his cell, his smile kept getting broader. There was an exciting prospect in the air, tangible to every prisoner in the facility. Mad Jimmy was the first. Who was next? Who would be the next inmate to suddenly have the balance of power switched for them? This question was painfully obvious on the faces of each and every guard who had not yet abandoned their post at Westvale. The wet stink of fear in the eyes of their captors was as intoxicating as freshly cooked bacon. Fear saturated Westvale, but it rarely originated from guards.

Jacob took a long, slow, drag off his cigarette, closed his eyes, and allowed his mind to swim with the possibilities, calculating odds and memorizing the best potential courses of action, so that it would be quick and natural when the time came.

First was the possibility that one of his inmates would suddenly become a Tek like Mad Jimmy did. In this case, Jacob's attitude towards the individual would be directly related to his assessment of their true feelings towards Jacob. Friendly Teks should immediately be convinced of Jacob's value, but only to the degree that they cared about Jacob at all. Unfriendly Teks, or those who were only friendly out of fear, would best be avoided. If unavoidable, they would require some quick words, distracting them long enough to shove something sharp in their eye. Eye wounds were highly efficient at ending combat before it began.

There was also the possibility that a guard became a Tek first. Jacob let out a deep lungful of smoke. It was a high probability that they would just continue to enforce the status quo. Which didn't change anything.

Jacob took another drag on his cigarette and blew smoke out between the teeth of his wide grin. Then there was the tantalizing chance that Jacob himself suddenly became a Tek. It was best to plan for that possibility as well.

It wouldn't be long now.

7 Days

It was around six o'clock in the evening as Thomas and Judy Bonner arrived at the 25th Annual Greenfield Moondog Festival. Parking in an empty grass field next to the fairgrounds, Tom and Judy got out, grabbed the two pies for Judy's annual entry into the pie-making contest, and meandered towards the entrance along with a gaggle of other townsfolk. Like everyone else nearing the gates, Tom greeted his friends and neighbors with the usual warm courtesy. This time, however, the attendees were not as easygoing as they should be at the annual fair. Smiles were strained; conversations were kept short and were often hushed. It was obvious that people had something else on their minds. Townsfolk that should be cheerful were fraught with hidden, suspicious fear.

Tom walked up to Elijah, an official Moondoggie, who was greeting people at the door in a bright orange vest. Tom had volunteered to be a Moondoggie once a few years back but had concluded that the other Moondoggies enjoyed arguing with each other more than they enjoyed actually working on the event.

"Howdy, Elijah," said Tom. Elijah was about Tom's age and had been part of the festival organizers for as long as Tom could remember.

"Evenin', Tom, evenin', Judy. So happy you made it," was Elijah's warm greeting.

"Actually, Elijah," Tom lowered his voice and leaned in, "I was surprised ya'll were still having it."

Elijah nodded and smiled to a few more festivalgoers as Judy took her pies and made her way to the Grand Pavilion to register for the bake-off. Elijah lowered his voice as well.

"Well, actually, Tom, there was some talk about that," he confided. "But hell, we haven't missed a festival since back before it was just called the Harvest Moon. And it's the 25th! Just because the rest of the world lost its gourd doesn't mean Greenfield needs to follow suit."

Tom couldn't see any flaws with that logic.

"Well alright, then. Here's to a good Moondog," Tom saluted as he let Elijah get back to his greetings. Tom entered the festival, scanning the main areas.

The big metal carnival rides were up and whirling about already, although they seemed strangely quiet without any screams coming from them, and Tom didn't see anyone on them. Probably the organizers were still getting them ready. The rip-off carnie games were already in full swing, as many shouts and excited squeals were coming from people winning stuffed animals. Tom made his way to the Harvest Field.

The Pea Pod-in-the-Haystack Hunt was always the kick-off for the official events of the Moondog festival. This event was always first so as to give the young contestants the benefit of twilight as they madly sifted through the hay for the hidden pea pod. Tom always enjoyed watching the frantic mess of children tear through the hay.

Tom grunted with disapproval as he noticed Erik Pullman, who Tom calculated to be at least fourteen years old, congregating with the other kids. Eric was really pushing the unwritten age limit for this event, in Tom's opinion. In addition to the fact that the prize for finding the pea was an obscenely large bag of candy, big kids always tended to trample the little kids in their enthusiasm.

Around fifteen kids total gathered in a huge ring around the pile of hay as their respective parental guardians claimed their positions at a safe viewing distance. The hay was artfully spread out on the ground in a small circular area, designed to ensure the search would not last longer than five minutes, yet allowing time for the adults to take pictures before heading for the food.

Tom couldn't help but get the feeling that the entire event was a little rushed. From the hasty corralling of the children to the minimal amount of whimsical banter from the Head Moondoggie announcing the start of the festival, it appeared that the whole town just wanted things to move along quickly so they could get through the festival without something weird happening.

"GO!" the Head Moondoggie hollered through his official bullhorn, and the kids all dashed towards the pile of hay in a cacophony of screams and giggles.

As Tom and the rest of the spectators watched, the 25th annual Moondog festival was undeniably touched by the weird. Every single child raced spontaneously to the exact same spot.

After the initial skull collisions between the two largest boys effectively took them out of the picture, the rest of the kids all reached for the same spot, but just as quickly they would snatch back their hands as if they had touched an open flame, looking at each other with hurt expressions on their faces.

The excitement of the crowd quickly dissipated with the realization that every contestant somehow knew exactly where the pea pod was, yet none of them seemed capable of grabbing it. The kids circled around the spot and stared wide-eyed at each other for a few seconds. Some of the younger ones started to cry. Erik Pullman sat up with his hand on his head and painfully swore.

Moments later, a little three-year-old blond girl named Cindy Hawkins, who was by far the youngest contender, finally arrived at the hay stack. Cindy waltzed unfazed through the legs of the other children, reached down, picked up the pea pod, held it up with an adorable smile on her face and proclaimed, "I win."

The parents all took that as their queue to swoop in and verify the health of their own, and to hurry their children away from the hay as if it was on fire. Erik and the boy he had collided with seemed to have suffered the most severe physical injuries, which was only a nasty lump on their respective noggins. Cindy's mother immediately snatched the pea pod from her daughter's hand and threw it away as if it were diseased. Cindy started to cry.

"And the winner, uh, of, uh the pea hunt," stammered the Head Moondoggie, "is Cindy." The organizer quickly turned off his bullhorn, turning to serious conversations with his fellow Moondoggies.

Tom, like the rest of the adults without a horse in the race, mostly just stood and watched, but was also trying to figure out what had just happened. Eavesdropping on parent inquisitions about the pea pod was not so easy, as most kids were flustered and most parents were terrified that something had happened to their precious babies. Tom caught sight of a kid by the name of Danny, who as older than most kids but not so old as to have knocked heads with the two boys who had led the charge. Danny's parents were apparently not around, as he was moving away towards the carnie games by himself.

Tom saw his chance and caught up to Danny.

"Hey Danny, how did ya know where the pod was?" Tom called out to him.

Danny turned and squinted back at Tom, obviously happy that someone had finally asked him about it.

"Didn't you?" was his prepared response.

Tom stopped in his tracks and frowned as he thought about this for a moment. Did he? He remembered glancing at the haystack earlier. If he had charged towards the haystack with the rest of the youngsters, would his first instinct have been to go for that exact same spot?

Happy with the reaction, Danny turned to leave.

"Fair enough. Well, then why didn't you grab it?" asked Tom.

In response, Danny got a nervous look on his face, turned, and quickly walked away. It was going to be an interesting night.

Tom grabbed a corn dog from a yellow and red mobile vendor and made his way towards the bake-off to meet up with Judy. The carnival rides remained empty. Folks must not feel like being thrilled.

"Over here, Judy!" waved Helen over the top of the crowd.

The Grand Pavilion, where the annual Moondog Bake-Off was being held, was slowly filling with people, although most of them were there to set up booths selling a wide assortment of this and that. The bake-off was in the corner, and the contestants were busy preparing their pies for display.

Helen was a friend of Judy's, although Tom liked to call her Judy's nemesis. In the bake-off as well as in any other cooking contests, formal or familiar, Helen presented stiff competition for Judy.

"Well, hello there Helen, fancy meeting you here," was Judy's opening quip.

Helen, who could always be counted on to be wearing some strange hat, smiled tersely and went back to setting up.

"Do you know who the judge is this year?" inquired Judy as she unpacked her two pies along with their presentation platter.

"Well, I heard that two already declined, but Miss Elly had popped her hand up," answered Helen, her oversized peacock feather waggling over her head.

"Oh, that's nice. She should be a good judge," Judy said. Elly was a popular, if not recent, addition to the community. With short black hair and barely in her thirties, she didn't have any longstanding feuds or friendships to affect her impartiality.

Judy paused. Considering her next to fantastic streak in the kitchen, this contest hardly seemed fair. Judy's already-famous rhubarb pie was absolutely perfect this time.

"I have to tell you Helen," said Judy. "I think I've got the bake-off all locked up this year," Judy said, smiling modestly as she put the final touches on her presentation.

Judy thought Helen said something, and thought she caught something shimmery in Helen's direction.

"What?" said Judy as she turned to Helen, who was staring at her.

"What?" asked Helen.

"What did you say?" asked Judy.

"I didn't…say anything," was Helen's broken response. This was an insincere comment if Judy ever heard one. Helen was being weird.

"What is it?" asked Judy. "You sound off."

Helen quickly shook the curious expression from her face, returned to tending to her own pie and replied, "I think maybe one of us is in for a surprise."

"Agreed," smiled Judy, turning back to her submission and checking to see if she forgot anything. This was standard Helen cattiness.

Soon the pies were all lined up on the elevated presentation table as young Elly prepared the official taste-walk down the line. Judy's pie was towards the end, Helen's was before hers.

Not needing silence, the audience continued their excited murmur as Elly used a fork on a slice of the first contestant's pie. Judy knew it couldn't be as good as hers, but Elly's reaction was absurd. Elly's eyes rolled back, she shot out her hand to steady herself, and closed her eyes as she chewed. Somehow Judy knew this was Mrs. Peabody's pie, and couldn't believe how over-the-top the "impartial" judge was acting.

The crowd grew quieter as the judge's curious reaction draw uneasy looks. Mrs. Peabody beamed with smugness as Miss Elly came to her senses and regained some composure. No longer the picture of poise, she scribbled a bunch of notes in her book and tentatively advanced to the second pie.

Somehow Judy also knew the baker of the next pie. This time it was Ken McDouglas, a first time pie competitor. Judy immediately found him in the crowd as he watched Miss Elly with a wide grin.

Much more nervously this time, the judge cautiously took a bite of the next pie, carefully chewing. This time, Miss Elly straightened and jotted down a few scribbles on her clipboard.

As she was about to proceed to the next pie, suddenly Miss Elly stopped.

"Oh!" Elly exclaimed as her face flushed.

"Oh my!" Elly said, dropping her clipboard to the ground, and clutching her stomach. "Oh my word!" she said, rushing off the stage and into the crowd.

"Hot damn!" laughed Ken McDouglas, as he slapped his hands together.

"What the hell did you do?" demanded a woman standing next to Ken.

"I tell ya' what!" laughed Ken. "If she don't say that was the best damn pie she ever had, she a' lyin'!"

Moondoggie officials rushed over to the judge. Chaos ensued.

Over the course of the next thirty minutes several things became clear. First off, Elly was fine but apparently had a literal orgasm on the stage and was mortified beyond belief. Second, nobody else dared to try Ken's pie, let alone the rest of the pies. Helen and Judy exchanged sad glances as the announcer blared over the top of the commotion that the bake-off was officially cancelled.

Tom found Judy exiting the Grand Pavilion dejectedly carrying some uneaten pies.

"What happened?" asked Tom.

"The pies were too good," said Judy. "The contest was cancelled and nobody even took a bite of my rhubarb masterpiece."

Tom looked around at a very sparsely populated Moondog Festival. A few short hours in, the festival would normally just be getting rolling, but now it looked like most folks had already left. Tom looked over to the carnival games and saw a number of booths shutting down.

"We should just go," said Judy to Tom. "It's just too much."

"You'd think the carnies at least would stick it out," said Tom.

Tom purposefully walked over to the booths and approached a greasy-looking man spinning an iron rod lowering his awning. The carnival operators were the few people from out of town that nobody knew.

"Why are you closing? The festival just started," Tom asked.

"Fuck this. I ain't losing my shirt," said the man, continuing his task without looking at Tom.

Tom kept staring at the man, trying to decipher what he said.

"Look," said the carnie, finally stopping and turning towards Tom.

"I watched four booths give out all their top prizes in less than an hour. Fucking kids knocked over three bottles with one throw, sacks on targets, and fuck me, the rings..." the man trailed off and went back to shutting down.

"You mean the kids were winning?" Tom said with a grin. Tom found this hilarious, considering the rip-off booths usually spent every year stealing money from poor kids bad at physics. "They got to win sometimes, don't they?"

"Fuck you," said the carnie. "You wouldn't be laughing if you saw them rings fall on those bottle tops. Fuck you and fuck this fucked up town."

Taken aback by so much hostility, Tom tipped his hat to the man and turned away to walk back towards Judy, who was heading back towards the parking lot. The normal routine after the pie contest was that Judy would pack her stuff in the car and come find Tom, but Tom agreed it would probably be best if they left too. The big rides had stopped moving. Some of them looked like they were getting ready to pack up as well.

As Tom left with the rest of the sad attendees, he saw a wild-eyed Edgar shuffling up to him. Edgar looked terrible, or at least, more so than usual. He was pale and his eyes looked bloodshot. Tom braced himself for the smell.

"I saw one, Tom! I saw one!" Edgar babbled as he got close. "I mean, I think it was one. I donna know what one looks like."

Tom was at a loss.

"Edgar, slow down, what did you see?"

"You know, a Moondog. Course, I never seen a real one before, so mebbie it wasn't one. Ya ever seen one?"

The Edgar aroma hit Tom's nostrils like a truck and distracted him. At first, Tom thought Edgar was talking about the festival organizers, but it was clear he was talking about something else.

"You mean, like, a dog?" asked Tom.

"Naw, it wadn't no dog. It was big and moony. It was a Moondoggie, I swear. I bet it's been dem that's been howlin too," Edgar stated, scratching his scraggly beard.

"Edgar, there is no such thing as a Moondoggie," Tom said has he rubbed his eyes. He wasn't sure where to start with this.

"Hey, just cause you ain't never seen one don't mean dey ain't real," Edgar stated confidently. "I didn't think they were real either."

Having gotten his answer, Edgar walked away again, and as usual, Tom was relieved to not be in smelling distance of him again.

As Tom met Judy at the car, he turned back to look at the festival. Aside from a few dozen teenagers and organizers, the 25th Annual Greenfield Moondog Festival seemed to be over. Tom wondered with sadness whether there would be a 26th.

7 DAYS

It was a brisk, sunny afternoon in Seattle, and the streets were packed with people. Keith Pennison headed East from Pike Place Market, along the busy downtown sidewalk, lost in his thoughts and harboring the same sense of dread that had been plaguing him for the past week.

Nothing made sense, and worse, he wasn't sure it would ever start to. He had no idea why he could move things with his mind, he had no idea what it had to do with the strange phenomena making daily headlines, and he had no idea where it was all leading. The only thing Keith felt for sure was that, given his newfound talents, he should be doing something, and probably doing something fast.

Keith waited for a walk signal in small group of pedestrians at the street corner. Two plump, middle-aged ladies, wearing moderately stylish felt jackets and bubbly expressions, were discussing the recent mass desertion of the freeway systems. Both ladies always rode the bus and thought the freeway commuter lifestyle was insanity all along. No doubt the speed of their chatter was perfected on the bus. All around him, all around town, all around the world, people were buzzing with excitement. Something very different was happening, and their generation was lucky to be a part of it. It was scary, yes, but there was a sense that everyone was all in it together, whatever it was.

Keith did not share their enthusiasm. Looking straight ahead, he casually reached out with his mind, caressing the exterior of the leather, pleather, polyester and cotton jackets of the bystanders around him. Keith was not part of the crowd gossiping about the world. He was the gossip.

Keith's mind returned to his role in all of this as the light changed and he began crossing the street with the crowd. Did he have an obligation to tell the world what he could do in hopes of furthering humanity's understanding? Keith didn't think so. Even if coming forward to help spread knowledge was the right thing to do, he really had no knowledge to give. Regardless, Keith had no intention of spending this special time hooked up to monitors and discussing things with scientists. He had watched the internet for signs of others who had his powers, and it was clear they were out there. It was also clear that the others like him felt as he did, for he had yet to hear a public statement from anyone.

As Keith walked down the sidewalk towards the entrance of the Westlake mall, he saw a massive crowd of people gathered around a street performer. Keith could not see the performer, but what he did see made him stop in his tracks, alongside most of the other people walking next to him.

At the center of the crowd, above gaping, upturned faces, two small blue and red plastic balls were floating. As Keith watched them, they made a very slow arc and Keith saw a third ball float up from the performer and continue in a circle after the others.

Keith's expression matched those around him. Shock. Every pedestrian who walked by and saw the floating balls either stopped dead in their tracks and stared or moved to try and get a better view. So many people had stopped that the sidewalks were running out of room and the horns of angry motorists were being drowned out by the swelling crowd.

Keith was not shocked by the floating balls, but he was absolutely floored by the brazenness of the display. Here was someone with his same power throwing caution to the wind and boldly showing every passer-by exactly what he was capable of. Keith absolutely had to see this person. Unfortunately, everybody else wanted to see the performer as well.

After about a minute of rude pushes and dirty looks, Keith was a meager two rows closer than he was before, and he realized he needed a different plan. Keith was never very good at being pushy, and he knew he would probably only gain a few more rows before people refused to move.

Keith steadied himself and reached out with his mind to feel in front of him. His experience at the coffee shop had taught him that the flesh of others was a sensation that shouldn't be taken lightly. He struggled to sort through the riot of sensory information and focus on his goal. There was an almost infinite amount of information available about any object, and it was easy to lose focus in the process. Keith explored the crowd in front of him carefully, keeping the touch as topical as possible.

The man to the front-left of Keith had a thin, bony arm, slightly wrinkled and mostly covered with a layer of white hair. The muscles were wiry and tough, there was tension all throughout them, and the bones themselves felt uptight. The man's clothes were old and soiled, and the side of his chest was equally emaciated.

The woman to the front-right had a large, gelatinous arm, mostly made up of saggy fat deposits. Her muscles were larger than those of the thin man, but still seemed disproportionably small compared to the rest of her arms.

Keith put aside the revolting feelings of flesh, bone, and clothes and gently pressed against the arms of the two people in front of him, opening up a path. He accompanied it with a real, physical push by his arm to make the movement look more natural.

The two spectators, already on guard because of Keith's earlier attempts to muscle ahead, both stared in surprise as Keith squeezed through their unexpected gap. The large woman looked at Keith, back at her arm, and then dismissed him with an audible "hmmph!"

The wiry man, however, stared back and forth from Keith to his arm and back again with wide eyes. Keith realized that the man was well aware of the physics involved when people shove each other in a crowd. A lightweight person knows how to keep his feet moving and let the pushing force transfer from person to person. They also knew that a person's arm doesn't just suddenly move sideways without weight behind it.

Keith lowered his head as he watched the old man's reaction out of the corner of his eye. He needed another, less conspicuous plan, though he wondered if the street performer up ahead would have simply raised his hands and parted the sea of people.

Distancing himself from the skinny man, who was now watching his every move, he reached out again, this time to the sleeves of his own pullover, firmly grabbing them with his mind. Then he simply nudged the people in front of him out of his way with his sleeves, which now had considerably more power than his arms did. Keith was careful not to send anyone flying, since this morning's tests confirmed he could pick up two full trash bags with little difficulty.

Keith still received some funny looks, but this time they were mostly just dirty looks. He found that if he could nudge somebody, and then just slip by onto the next person, people weren't quite sure who needed the glaring.

Keith arrived at the front row and did one final squeeze to get a good look at the center of attention. Everybody was clapping as the man held his arms straight out as the colorful balls orbited his head.

The performer was a vagrant. He was dressed in some sort of dark blue jumpsuit, which had even darker stains scattered about on it. He had a bald, pasty white head with long, black hair frayed in the back and a long, black beard to match. In front of him sat a top hat, quaintly upside-down, and overflowing with bills. As Keith watched, various people nervously made their ways to the hat and made generous offerings.

The man's manner was positively silly. He smiled and waved as the seemingly magical balls hovered about him. He made dramatic hand movements as the balls danced around in the air, guiding them to and fro. Judging by the man's actions and his top hat, Keith figured the man probably really was just a homeless street performer, who happened to be cashing in on his newfound abilities.

Keith looked around again at the crowd, taking note of a cop standing in awe, and several professional businessmen, all full of wonder and amazement. Nobody was trying to burn this man as a witch, no government agencies were swooping in to drag him away; everyone was just curious and fascinated. Keith thought maybe he was taking himself too seriously, and that he wasn't actually in any danger of becoming a lab rat if his powers were exposed.

The performer made an upward motion with his hand and one of the balls flew towards the sky at an impossible speed. He repeated the gesture and one after another, the balls went shooting towards the heavens, each departure met with "ooos" and "aahs" by the crowd. After an impossible number of seconds, the balls began falling down and were all caught in mid-air by the performer's invisible hands. The crowd cheered, the man bowed, and more bills were either stuffed into his hat or laid on top of the pile.

Keith decided to try to learn whatever he could from this man. He reached out and felt one of the floating balls with his own mind. There didn't seem to be anything unusual about the ball itself, nor could he feel any strange forces around it. It was simply a moving ball. The performer did not notice Keith's probing.

Keith decided he was going to grab the ball with his mind himself and see what the man's reaction would be. He picked the ball closest to him, felt it, and then strongly locked it in place with his mind.

Instantly, the performer turned and stared directly at Keith, mouth hanging open. The other balls dropped to the pavement.

In the same instant, Keith felt a weird kind of electricity, as if he was grabbing onto the ends of a car battery, if the electricity was somehow made up of thoughts. First and foremost, he knew the bum thought the ball should proceed downwards, but it was as if Keith could feel the rest of the man's thoughts behind it, which ranged from amusement to contempt to how he was a little bit hungry.

Disappointment rippled audibly through the crowd, which had just noticed the new player entering the game. Those nearest began backing away from Keith.

Realizing that his cover had been blown, Keith released the ball and the strange feelings immediately vanished. Keith nervously looked around feeling a rising tide of panic as all eyes seemed to be on him.

The performer was unperturbed and walked right up in front of Keith.

"Hey there, I'm Rupert," said the man with a toothy smile, never taking his eyes from Keith's.

"Hi. Uh, Keith," managed Keith, unsure of whether he should have used a fake name and overwhelmed with thoughts of bolting. The one-man show had become a two-man act, and all eyes were scrutinizing every move they made.

The ball that Keith had grabbed, still hanging in mid-air where Keith had grabbed it, flew up and away as if someone had thrown it over their shoulder. Keith struggled to regain his composure, not used to being the center of attention.

"What say we go grab a cup of joe? My treat," Rupert grinned widely at Keith again. At this range, he could smell Rupert's smell of old sweat and urine. It was not pleasant.

Noticing Keith's look of apprehension, Rupert glanced over his shoulder at the muttering, whispering herd. Still grinning, he walked over to his hat, gave the bills a final stuff, and put the cap on his head, leaving a small pile of cash and shedding bills all over the place. He started walking back over to Keith, who was nervously looking at the ground, and paused with an incredulous expression.

"What … are you serious? Them?" Rupert jerked a dismissive thumb at the crowd. "You worried about them?"

Keith didn't know what to say. This man must be mad. He took a step closer to Rupert and tried his best to whisper, "I don't think they'll let us have coffee in peace, uh, friend."

Rupert looked at the group of wide-eyed onlookers, half of which appeared to be livestreaming the event, then looked back at Keith, and smiled.

"Aw, no, they'll lose us." He grinned at Keith, who was trying to figure out how one would accomplish telekinetic crowd control.

"Come with me." Rupert strode forward and grabbed Keith around the shoulders, spun him around, and escorted him through the mass of bodies. Keith stumbled alongside Rupert, who was at least a full foot taller than him.

As Keith tried to hold back his gag reflex at Rupert's sickening stench, he started noticing that all eyes were no longer on them. Phones seemed to wildly search for them. He figured that those in the back of the crowd simply didn't know what the two looked like, but it seemed like those that were most eager to follow them seemed to be losing track of them as well. Keith was more puzzled than before. He was sure they would be followed by a herd of fascinated people and had no idea why the crowd wasn't sticking to them like glue.

"Stop it," said Rupert.

"Stop what?" Keith asked, politely removing Rupert's arm and walking on his own.

"Never mind," mumbled Rupert.

By the time they arrived at the Starbucks at the end of the street, Keith was astonished to find that the entire crowd had indeed lost them, just as Rupert had predicted. Walking into Starbucks as anonymous customers, Keith was eager to learn how Rupert had accomplished this feat.

After Keith endured a scene where Rupert jovially and somewhat condescendingly threw a wad of cash at the barista, the two sat down on the patio with Keith's tall Chai Latte and Rupert's venti Caramel Frappuccino with extra caramel.

Keith could barely contain his excitement.

"Ok, so you have to tell me how that all happened back there. I know how to move stuff just like you, but I wouldn't know where to begin if a mob was after me," Keith confessed. Here was someone who might know more than him, someone who could teach him things; someone who maybe had some answers.

Rupert slowly took a long slurp of his monstrous beverage. He wiped some whipped cream off of his matted beard and smiled at Keith.

"No," replied Rupert, as his grin grew wider.

Keith was hurt. "No?" he asked.

"Look kid, life is all about experience. I can't ruin it for you. It wouldn't be fair to you. You'll learn; you'll all learn."

Keith was beginning to think Rupert's life on the street had made him a bit cynical. He was starting to think that Rupert was just enjoying feeling superior to those who had previously pulled rank on him.

"Tell ya what, kid," Rupert leaned forward in his chair. "You tell me what you know and I'll tell you what you need to know."

Keith considered this for a moment, and decided it was a fair bargain.

"Well, I know I can move stuff with my mind. And I can feel things before I move them, as if I somehow can feel what they are." Keith looked at Rupert, who made a motion for him to continue.

"And?"

"That's about all I really can say I know. I don't know why I'm special, I don't know what it has to do with all the weirdness in the papers, and I don't know what I'm supposed to do," Keith admitted.

Rupert grinned again and leaned back in his chair. "So, you think you're special? Aw, come on, you know more than that."

Keith didn't like Rupert's belittling manner. Rupert really seemed to be enjoying this, and Keith didn't feel like playing twenty questions with him.

"So what do I need to know?" Keith said flatly.

Rupert pondered this for a second, took another big slurp of pure caramel, and then turned to Keith.

"Remember when you touched my balls?" he asked.

Keith couldn't help but smile at the crazy person.

"Well, uh, yes," he replied.

"Well, guess what Keith, my man?" Rupert stood up. "You're touching everybody's balls!" roared Rupert as he scooped up his drink. He turned and crashed off the patio laughing hysterically, as if he just said the funniest thing in the world. "It's a fucking ball fondling party! Bahahaha!" cackled Rupert as he careened into people, sloshing Frappuccino all down the sidewalk.

Keith sipped on his Chai Latte for a few stunned minutes. He was horribly disappointed but wanted to extract the most information out of the situation. Rupert obviously knew more about what was going on, but he didn't feel it was important enough to share his knowledge. Either the crazy bum was selfish, or maybe it really didn't matter. Instead of stressing out about what the future held, maybe he should just learn to enjoy himself like Rupert was expertly doing.

Keith sipped on his latte and checked his news feed. Banks were reportedly no longer safe places to keep cash, as "Teks" kept strolling out with it, and there was little anyone could do to stop them. "Teks" was the media's new name for telekinetic people. Somehow nobody got it confused with technician. Keith tried to refocus on what Rupert had told him.

So, he was "touching everybody's balls," whatever that meant. He didn't feel like he was messing with everybody's daily routine. When he had grabbed Rupert's ball, he had felt something really strange, as if he was grabbing Rupert. Not Rupert's body, but more like his mind. Was he therefore grabbing everybody's mind and not knowing it? More disturbingly, was he the only one grabbing balls or was his balls being grabbed, too? Keith wished he had been able to ask Rupert more questions. In fact, he wasn't sure why he had let Rupert walk away without following him.

Keith cursed Rupert under his breath. Whatever was going on was too important to speak in riddles about.

6 Days

Claire Nelson sped down the fast lane, trying her hardest to identify what exactly all the Freeway Fear fuss was about. Poor Adam was always a wreck when he got home, and Claire wished she could somehow sympathize or at least figure out exactly what was rattling him.

Claire's Mustang approached a silver BMW ahead in the fast lane. Anxious for any kind of interaction, she delicately stepped on the gas, approaching 75 in a 60 zone, but the BMW got out of her way long before she caught up to it. Far from being threatening in any way, motorists seemed like they were being extra nice to her. Her drive was not scary. It never was.

The high-pitched whine of a crotch rocket caught Claire's attention and she glanced in her rearview mirror to see a yellow helmeted figure on some Kawasaki deathtrap weaving through the traffic behind her. Claire could not deny the thrill of a fast ride on a strong engine, but for her, motorcycles on freeways crossed the line from awesome to suicidal.

The rider obviously had zero Freeway Fear like she did, so Claire thought maybe here was a chance to maybe see how Adam felt about other drivers. Claire slowed down to just over the speed limit, matching the speed of the surrounding traffic, as the bike closed in fast.

A split second later, the fast-moving object was past, zooming through the traffic at an incredibly dangerous speed, even by crotch rocket standards. Claire checked to see if she could sense anything from the crazy driver like her husband was always complaining about. Nothing. In fact, trying to make any sudden turns seemed impossible as the thing raced by. Everyone was probably trying not to make any sudden moves that the biker hadn't planned for.

Claire's morning commute continued to be disappointingly normal. There was a moment, when she was merging, that a VW to her left braked hard to give her an absurd amount of room to merge, but other than that, the drive was uneventful, quite possibly more boring than usual. Almost too much courtesy on the road.

Claire thought about what the news had been saying about the Freeway Fear as she arrived at the Clark Center building and got on the elevator. She had never considered herself an aggressive driver, but she couldn't deny the fact that slowpoke drivers tended to piss her off.

It wasn't that Claire minded being labeled as aggressive—quite the opposite, most of the time "aggressive" was synonymous with "winner." Being aggressive behind the wheel, however, carried with it a social stigma of being the causer of all accidents. Claire thought this commonly held theory was completely backwards. People not paying attention caused accidents, not assertive people who were focused on what they were doing. Gertrude made Claire confess that she didn't suffer from the slightest twinge of the Freeway Fear, so of course it was now common knowledge around the office. Claire wasn't offended by the "aggressive driver" label, but she was a little hurt that this was unsurprising to all of her coworkers.

As Claire exited the elevator, Gertrude spotted Claire's arrival out of the corner of her eye and plotted a course to intercept.

"Oh hon…" was Gertrude's greeting as she tailed Claire into her office.

Attempting to evade the *Gertrude in the Morning* show was futile. Something was up, and there was no escaping the fact that she was about to hear all about it.

"Hey Claire, notice anything different about the office, do ya?" Gertrude asked.

Claire debated whether she could go on pretending there wasn't a large and loud woman at her door as she settled at her desk. In the end, the fact that Gertrude was waiting for a response before continuing her speech meant it was probably something important.

Claire glanced past the sizeable obstruction in her door.

"Lloyd's not in yet?" Claire guessed.

"Yes, but that's not all," Gertrude advanced into Claire's office, counting matter-of-factly on her fingers. "Amir left weeks ago, Cheryl is still out sick with the flu, or the stomach thing, or whatever excuse she gave you, and now Lloyd called me this morning to say that he is never coming back!"

Gertrude paused for the magnitude of the situation to dawn on Claire, who obviously wasn't getting it.

"There's only me and Carl left on the floor, Claire!" Gertrude whined.

Claire listened quietly for a moment. She didn't hear any ringing or any talking.

"Are you guys busy?" Claire asked Gertrude.

"Well, no, but-" Gertrude began.

"Well okay, then let me know when you are, and I'll help you guys out. In the meantime, I'll get corporate on the line and figure out what they want to do about people not coming in."

Though Gertrude's face was full of disappointment at the level of alarm Claire showed, the idea of corrective action seemed to appease her, and Claire's "go away" demeanor indicated she should leave. With a barely audible harrumph, Gertrude turned and walked back to her desk.

Having only two employees show up for work was, indeed, much more cause for alarm than Claire allowed Gertrude to see. In fact, there had already been several upper-level meetings on the subject, and Corporate was preparing to shut down operations unless employee attendance went back up. Managers had already been advised to allow absent employees to come back to work without consequences, no questions asked.

This whole situation would have been a much larger catastrophe if call volume had not dropped off the chart as well. According to the numbers, two-employee coverage sounded just about right. People just didn't seem to be very concerned about their cell phone bill when the internet was full of videos of people moving things with their minds.

5 Days

Judy Bonner stood in the kitchen staring at the pile of groceries she had purchased earlier in the day. It was time to start making dinner, and as Tom was preparing his daily musing-time on the porch, Judy was wondering what in the world she was about to cook.

It was a chicken dish, for sure, but there was also some bacon, some onions, and even a bottle of red wine. Judy grabbed the wine and inspected it. Pinot Noir. When she picked it off the wine rack earlier today, she was mostly looking for a good price, but then again, did it need to be Pinot Noir? The shopping trip was strange, but no stranger than this other idea she had.

Judy closed her eyes as Tom puffed on the porch in the other room. All she needed was to focus on that fact that tonight's dinner was going to be amazing. That little thought seemed all that was required to give her hands the direction of what to do next. Somehow, it didn't matter that she didn't know when to add the wine if all she thought about was how great the dinner was going to be. Somehow, the wine would get added.

Judy opened her eyes and looked again at the stack of onions, mushrooms, vegetables and spices.

"Tom? Can you come in here a moment?" called Judy.

Tom walked over with beer in hand.

"What is it, hon?" asked Tom.

"Can you watch me cook tonight? You know, just make sure I don't burn the house down or anything silly," asked Judy.

With a confused look on his face, Tom opened his mouth to reply, but then froze when he saw Judy pull out a large black sock from her back pocket, wrap it around her eyes and start tying it in the back.

"Are you kidding me, Judy?" Tom asked incredulously.

"Why not?" said Judy, giving the knot on her blindfold one final tug. "I already don't even know what I'm cooking, why not just let my hands do the work? It's like I barely need to pay attention anymore." Judy's hands were already off and running with prep work.

"But…the knives!" protested Tom as Judy snatched a kitchen knife out of a drawer and began cutting and splitting the onions.

"And…the flames!" exclaimed Tom as Judy lit a burner before placing a pot of water on it.

"I know, it's totally nuts Tom," Judy said, turning a blindfolded face towards Tom's horrified expression as her hands were opening the chicken and getting out a plastic bag. "But if I just trust that tonight's dinner will be incredible, my hands can do no wrong!"

There was a quiet pause coming from Tom's direction as Judy felt herself pulling out a few small bowls, probably for mixing.

"If you say so, Judy. I hope you know what you're doing," resigned Tom, as Judy pulled out a sauté pan with her left hand and snapped the gas on a second burner with her right. The way her hands moved bordered on unnatural. Not simply ambidextrous, they completely disregarded starting and finishing tasks, with a few stirs here and a pan shake there.

There was master-chef-level slicing of vegetables, multiple sautés, and of course the wine, all ending up in a Dutch oven on the center rack at 325 degrees.

Judy turned her face to Tom.

"How'd I do?" Judy smiled.

"Well, the kitchen is a complete mess, but nothing burned down. You really moved like you were possessed. You sure you don't got no evil spirits in ya?" Tom sounded like he was only half-joking.

Judy took off her blindfold and looked around.

"Oh dear. I sure wish I could clean like I can cook."

Two hours later, Judy pulled the dish out of the oven and still had almost another hour of sauce thickening and straining before the exotic meal was finally ready.

The Bonners both stuffed themselves to the point of stomach aches, but the meal was so savory, it felt like a crime not to gorge as much as possible while it was hot. The experience was magical at first, but when the plates were bare, it was a touch frightening to both of them. What if Judy cooked a meal so magically tasty that they physically couldn't stop eating until their stomachs burst? They both agreed Judy should tone it down, and by all means, she should keep her eyes open while she cooked.

4 Days

Adam Nelson rode happily in the back of Janine's minivan, next to Harold from IT, feeling stupid for taking so long to sign up for the carpool. There was still something off about the highways, but somehow riding in the car with his coworkers felt amazing.

The relief was also shared.

"You okay there, Janine?" Harold said from behind his thick glasses and even thicker black mustache. It was his first day in the carpool, and he wore a grin from ear to ear.

"It's fine, Harold. I told you, driving is just as easy as riding," Janine called back. A small-framed woman with long, straight hair, Adam wasn't sure what department Janine was from, but he knew she had been carpooling for over a week now.

Adam hardly knew these people, but he had seen them around the office. He may have talked on the phone with Harold before. They had already made one stop to drop off Stephanie, and Adam's house was next.

A blue pickup truck cut in front of Janine and a shadow of a feeling flickered across Adam's thoughts. Adam was forced to admit his Freeway Fear wasn't gone completely, but it was certainly dialed down by several orders of magnitude.

Harold turned his husky Indian smile towards Adam.

"You still feel it, right?" Harold asked.

"Yeah, I think so," pondered Adam. "I just don't feel like I'm going to die because of it."

"I know, right?" beamed Harold, turning back towards the front.

Adam looked out the window and tried to focus on the little movements of the cars beside him, the ones that were so unnerving when driving solo. There was still something weird about them, as if they were whispering things to Adam's subconscious that he shouldn't be able to hear. Something about the drivers.

"124, right?" Janine called back to Adam.

"Yes. That one. Thanks," Adam replied.

Janine flipped on her right blinker and again there was a barely noticeable flash of something coming from the car to their right, as if someone far away had shouted some protest or curse, but they were too far away to be heard.

Adam turned and saw Janine hiding a sly smile as she merged in front of the car that had slowed to let her in.

"It's like we overrule them," she said, and Adam felt there must be some truth to that. It was like they were dealing with the Freeway Fear together, and the act of sharing the Fear made them all much stronger against it.

After a few more minutes, the gang was stopped in front of the Nelson's townhome and Adam grabbed his laptop bag as the sliding door of the minivan mechanically slid open to let him out.

"And you two are good on your own?" Adam asked. In his two days of carpooling, he was always with at least three people. Although still a ghost of the solo Fear, he was sure it was more noticeable the fewer occupants remained in the car.

Harold shot a worried look towards Janine, who smiled back at him.

"Aw yeah, you only need two to tango," she chided as Adam stepped out of the car.

"And you're going to be okay after you drop Harold off?" Adam asked. Janine stopped smiling.

"I can take backroads. They're really not bad at all," she said as the side door slid closed between them. Adam didn't recall noticing the Fear on the short trip to the grocery store last weekend.

As Janine drove off, Adam once again thanked his lucky stars for the carpool. While his first day had him almost weeping with relief, this second day he could get back to appreciating his arrival home to his family without trauma.

Adam sauntered up the short steps to the front door of the Nelson's townhome and walked inside. Claire was in the kitchen on the main ground floor, working on dinner. They usually tried to share dinner responsibility, but since Claire got home earlier than him, he was often just the dishwasher.

"Well, you look good," said Claire as Adam walked in. She was obviously preoccupied with dinner, glancing back and forth between Adam and the oven.

Cory was busy playing video games in the living room to the left of the entryway as Adam deposited his keys and loosened his tie.

"Well, I feel good, Claire. I can't believe I waited so long to sign up," Adam said as he crossed the living room to give her a quick peck on the cheek.

"What's for dinner?" asked Adam, smelling something pungent.

"Smells like butt!" called Cory.

"Cory!" scolded Claire halfheartedly, turning back to Adam. "Yeah, sorry, cooking is not my superpower," she said as she turned and crouched back down to peer into the oven. "How about you, babe? Are you magic yet?"

"Nope, sorry, still as normal as the next guy."

"Well, the government is completely losing their shit," Claire said quietly, still facing the oven. Adam hadn't checked the news today.

"Really? Do I want to know?" asked Adam.

"No, not really. Just trying to control everything as usual, and I don't think they can control this. And… something else," Claire's voice lowered as she eyed Cory and motioned Adam to come with him. The two casually sauntered into the pantry as noises from Cory's first-person shooter ensured they couldn't be heard.

"Monsters," said Claire, quietly.

"Monsters?" asked Adam, immediately thinking about Nessie. "Like in New York?"

"No, like kids who are afraid of monsters," Claire whispered. "Like, little kids who are afraid of monsters getting fucking murdered by actual monsters," Claire hissed. She was dead serious.

Adam was shocked. He had read about monsters becoming real but hadn't seen anything about kids.

"Read about it. Later. And don't tell Cory. I'm pretty sure he is over his 'monster-under-the-bed' phase, but the last thing we want to do is make him afraid of monsters again."

Claire walked back to the kitchen to check on her foul-smelling dinner, leaving Adam to process the news.

Cory heard his parents lower their voices and sneak into the pantry. Obviously, they wanted to talk about him behind his back.

Cory didn't care, though. Never mind this dumb game that his team was sucking all over, all he could think of was what he would do if he got superpowers. That ass-face Jeff would regret trying to touch him, that was for sure.

And nobody would ever call him Squeaker again.

4 Days

Jacob Christenson sat on the benches observing other inmates play basketball in the yard. The colossal waste of time known as exercise always provided ample opportunity to study his other inmates.

Jacob's bunkie Darrey sat to his left, one bench down. Lacking a spine himself, Darrey had come to understand the benefits of being close to Jacob. Naturally, there was the requisite violence when they first met, but by now Darrey knew his place well.

To the right of Darrey sat Little Fatty. Little Fatty was a small, round, obnoxious man, whom Jacob had utterly detested the moment he laid eyes on him. Jacob tried hard to pretend the little fat shit wasn't so close to him.

Jacob was watching Alberto, a big Mexican thug playing basketball. Alberto hated Jacob, which was amusing. Unfortunately, this meant that Jacob should probably kill Alberto before the dumb thug made a move against him. It was just the reality of stupid fucks who refused to understand who was in charge.

Alberto shoved a guy named Jesus to the ground while charging with the ball, yelling blame at Jesus for being in the way. Alberto always telegraphed his actions on his face. Predicting his next move would be easy, as long as you kept an eye on his dirty mug. The interesting part was guessing what sort of plan a man like that would dream up for Jacob. A shiv in the back would certainly match his style, but you could see the brute coming a mile away. Alberto was not sociable, and even among the Mexicans it was improbable someone would pull a stab job for him. Best to watch Alberto for any new friends.

Fatty was blathering about something.

"You gotta get dem when they like dat, ya know? You shoulda seen it, Jacob, sweet thing, gawd damn." Fatty was probably talking about his sexual conquests, or conquests he dreamed he had, or conquests he assumed his friends would find impressive. Fucking Fatty. Staring ahead and making it clear he wasn't listening, Jacob tried hard not to listen.

A skinny guy with a heavily tattooed face named Frisco strolled over behind the stands and casually sauntered up behind Jacob. Frisco was a reliable spreader of info, and his furtive glancing meant he had news. Jacob kept his eyes forward and waited as Darrey and Little Fatty straightened and regarded Frisco.

"Yo, it happened again. Like Jimmy," was Frisco's soft-spoken shocker of news, referring to Mad Jimmy's explosive Tek outburst.

Fatty jumped at the opportunity to run his mouth.

"Holy crap! Who? Did you see it? I didn't hear no lockdown. When? Did any C/Os get fucked up?" Fatty eagerly babbled.

"Kentner," whispered Frisco.

"Kentner?" exclaimed Fatty. "Who the fuck is Kentner?" Little Fatty turned towards Darrey who wore a similar confused expression.

"Quiet guy," Jacob stated, still watching Alberto. "Old guy. Mid-fifties. No friends." Jacob had been informed Kentner was neither threat nor ally when he arrived at Westvale nearly three years ago. Jacob had eventually confirmed this, ordering someone to kick Kentner's ass and then offering Kentner protection. Kentner's response to both tests was pathetic. Jacob suspected the guy was some sort of pacifist. "Not exciting."

Jacob turned his head slightly to Frisco, hoping fucking Fatty would shut his mouth for a fucking second. "What happened?"

Frisco launched into the story.

"Dude, the guy just got up and left," said Frisco. "Check it; we were just sitting in the chow hall, then Kentner gets up all fidgety-like, and says he's leaving. Everyone's laughing but then the guy walks right over to the door and it opens for him. Guards are flipping out, but they can't get near him."

Jacob's mind swam with possibilities, but his face remained undisturbed. There was a lot to unpack here, most importantly any similarities between Mad Jimmy and Kentner.

"But get this," Frisco continued. "The asshole was locking the doors after he went through. Like just to make sure nobody could rabbit with him."

"So he didn't fuck anyone up?" Fatty interjected. "Not even anyone who fucked with him?" Fatty tried to hide his sideways glance towards Jacob, which was irritating on so many levels. It was clear Fatty hated Jacob with a passion, yet somehow maintained the delusion that Jacob didn't know this.

"Naw," said Frisco, his eyes darting between Fatty and Jacob. "He just left."

Jacob turned his head to Fatty. "He's not talking to you," he said calmly.

Tilting back to Frisco as Fatty wore an indignant frown, Jacob asked, "What can you tell me about Kentner?"

Frisco thought a moment.

"Not much, Jacob," shrugged Frisco. "The guy was only two cages down from me, but I can't say I've ever heard so much as a peep from him. Liked books, I think."

This wasn't new. Jacob tried to think of anything else to ask Frisco.

Little Fatty couldn't help himself. "So, did he like, lift anything? You sure he was-"

"Shut up, Fatty," Jacob cut him off, quietly. Alarm spread over the faces of Darrey and Frisco as they straightened. But Little Fatty was focused on Jacob.

"Naw, see here, fuck you, Jacob," started Fatty. "I wanna hear the story and I got just as much right-"

Jacob quickly turned and brought his boot down hard, squashing Fatty's fat hand where it was resting on the aluminum bench. The little man squealed like the pig he was.

"I said, shut up," hissed Jacob slowly, his face close to Fatty's. Fatty probably didn't hear him over his own squealing and crying, as he scrabbled at Jacob's boot on his hand.

A couple of inmates seated on the benches near them paused their conversation and turned to watch the drama. A guard next to the court halfheartedly turned his head in their direction.

Jacob lifted his boot and returned to his seated position watching the game. Fatty pulled his crumpled hand to his chest and stood up, his face a fat red twist of anger and shame.

"Fuck you, Jacob," Fatty stammered as he backed away. "Just… fucking fuck you!" Fatty turned and retreated, clutching his hand, sniffling and mumbling to himself.

Jacob turned to Frisco as the rest of the yard resumed their own distractions.

"Thank you, Frisco," said Jacob. "Let me know if you find out anything else interesting about Kentner."

Frisco nodded and walked off.

Violence was never the first choice when it came to handling people. It was typically a risky move, even if one was skilled at combat, as Jacob was. But as with all actions, the reward sometimes outweighed the risk. In his second week as a resident of Westvale, a muscled jackass named Robinson had tried to mess with Jacob. Jacob didn't like his odds in a fist fight, so while waiting in the chow line one day, he had calmly turned, walked over to where Robinson was eating, leapt onto the thug's unsuspecting head and gouged one of Robinson's eyes out of its socket with the end of a plastic knife. Truthfully, the eyeball was more mangled than actually torn out, but it was the story that counted. After a few more story-worthy incidents, it became widely known that only a fool would try to fuck with Jacob Christenson. Jacob had no nickname at Westvale, he was simply Jacob.

Jacob and Darrey sat in silence for a few minutes, both pretending to watch the ball game.

The degree of uncertainty around these new incidents was unsettling to Jacob. Planning and predicting shivs, shanks, alliances, and betrayals was easy, but you only needed to watch a couple of minutes of news to see it was clear there was no defense against an angry Tek. The million-dollar question was naturally, "how does one become a Tek?"

This question only had a few clues so far. First, being a little bit nuts apparently increased your chances of becoming a Tek. Not that every nutjob had the power, or that every Tek was crazy, but having a few screws loose apparently greatly increased your chances of waking up one morning moving shit with your mind. Mad Jimmy was the kind of crazy who was never exactly sure where he was. That psycho probably belonged in a mental institution. Kentner, on the other hand, wasn't crazy at all, as far as anyone knew. A little quiet and thoughtful, but extremely predictable.

Jacob noticed Darrey was looking at him.

"Yes?" asked Jacob.

"You think it's a good idea, to, you know, keep on fucking with shits like Little Fatty?" asked Darrey.

Jacob smiled. Was Darrey suggesting Jacob do a complete restructuring of his entire social hierarchy at Westvale to base his connections on friendship as opposed to fear, to increase the likelihood of former inmate Teks choosing to aid him instead of squashing him like a bug?

This absurd notion had crossed Jacob's mind. Such a project would take at best months, at worst years, if such a thing were even possible, given his current level of infamy.

"Too late to stop now," answered Jacob with a smile. He had fast words and faster shivs prepared for a confrontation with a Tek, but that high-risk situation would best be avoided altogether.

One thing for sure was that everyone at Westvale was dreaming about what they would do if they got the power. Jacob knew what he would do. He would rule the mother-fucking world.

4 Days

Keith stepped out the front door of his apartment complex to wait for his Uber, nervously fidgeting his fingers as he prepared his latest experiment.

Living in downtown Seattle, only a few blocks from where he had worked, Keith hadn't seen the need to own a car, and, therefore, he hadn't personally experienced the biggest event that was making headlines today: The Freeway Fear. The monsters, the miracles, and all the rest of the extraordinary or bizarre tales had taken a back seat to this one big story, which, unlike the other stories, was readily visible to the general population.

The Freeway Fear first started popping up in Keith's news feed several weeks ago, but it had since become an international phenomenon. According to the news reports, there were two types of drivers: aggressive and defensive. While aggressive drivers were unaffected by the Fear, defensive drivers were becoming overwhelmed with this intangible terror anytime they drove on a freeway. The Freeway Fear allegedly only struck these poor souls when other cars were near, and usually only when they were traveling at high speeds.

Considering he never drove anywhere, Keith wondered what kind of driver he was as the rideshare app beeped an alert that his driver was near.

Steeling himself for action, Keith reached out with his mind to the car in front of him and lifted if off its suspension, the creaking inaudible over the noisy street in front of him. Such a feat would have been unthinkable for him a week before, but now it was just a mild strain, as if the heaviness of the object pulled his thoughts towards sleep. The news was reporting that the Freeway Fear had one thing in common with Keith's power; both were getting stronger.

A red Prius pulled up in front of Keith's apartment and he picked his way between the parked cars to the door.

Keith mused about what kind of driver would best facilitate his experiment. An aggressive Uber driver might not exhibit the Fear, but an erratic ride with a freaked out defensive driver didn't sound fun either. Keith figured defensive cab drivers probably were uncommon, even before all the weirdness.

"Keith?" asked the driver.

The driver was a rather chunky white man with a little hat that made him look like he came from the Bronx. According to Uber, his name was "Herb." To Keith's surprise, he appeared to wear a mildly excited expression, devoid of anything resembling fear.

"Uh huh," answered Keith as he got in.

"East side, eh?" was the question, gruff yet somehow cheery. Keith thought he detected a hint of east coast in Herb's accent, though if he was from New York, he had been gone a while.

"Yeah, Bellevue," answered Keith. The I-90 bridge across Lake Washington was a perfect example of a high-speed freeway, and he had one other experiment in mind for his trip back across the lake.

Herb smiled at something, presumably the length of the trip, and chirped the tires of his Prius to announce his entrance onto the downtown road.

Immediately Herb's level of aggression became clear. The man was impatient at lights, snuck closely by slow-moving vehicles, and, for the most part, took every chance he could to put his gas pedal to the floor—which of course necessitated his slamming on the brake pedal just as frequently.

Keith scrambled to hold onto something. Herb paid no attention to Keith, or to the sounds of his passenger crashing around in the back.

Preoccupied with his own safety, Keith suddenly remembered the purpose of the trip, which was to study the drive itself. Keith turned his attention to Herb.

Herb seemed to be trying to hide a toothy smile, practically a sneer. The Prius accelerated onto I-5, heading for I-90, and Keith watched as Herb gunned the puny Prius engine. This was not someone interested in making money; this was a guy who was enjoying his job. Keith wondered if Herb always had such a hoot while driving.

A sharp turn made Keith consider the probability of successfully catching the entire cab with his mind if it were to flip off the freeway due to Insane Uber Driver Piloting Error. He had considered Tek intervention beforehand, but this was not supposed to have been a serious possibility. Keith wished that he had come up with a better disaster plan.

"Not many people on the road these days, eh?" Keith ventured.

"Oh, it's been glorious," was Herb's immediate response. "Every jackass that shouldn't have been on the road in the first place shit his britches and caught himself a bus."

Keith contemplated how to respond to this as Herb glanced back at him through his rearview mirror, checking to be sure he hadn't offended his passenger.

"Are, uh, any of them still on the road? The, uh, the ones that shouldn't be there?" Keith ventured again.

"Not so much anymore," came the swift response. Herb seemed relieved that Keith didn't appear to take offence at his honesty or whine about his driving.

"You can always spot 'em, though, you can see 'em coming a mile away and let me tell you, it's best to steer well clear of those folks," warned Herb.

Herb's answers sounded as if he had talked about this before with his passengers. Keith surmised that just about anyone who employed Herb's services probably either wanted to talk about the Fear or they wanted to avoid the subject. Intrigued by Herb's responses and slightly more relaxed now that they were on the freeway and not erratically zipping through downtown, Keith moved to the middle of the back seat and leaned forward.

"If you see one of them, can you show me?" Keith asked over Herb's shoulder.

Herb took another glance in his rear-view. "Sure ..." There was a pause. "But uh, what's your interest?" As Keith considered his response, Herb added, "If we pass one, I ain't gettin' too close to it."

Keith hadn't expected his motives to be questioned. "Oh, I'm just curious. I heard they are real dangerous." Keith hoped his attempt at taking Herb's side wasn't too transparent.

It wasn't.

"Hell yeah, them suckers' are dangerous!" Herb nodded emphatically. "If you even look at them funny, they're liable to run themselves into a goddam telephone pole!" Herb's exasperation struck Keith as a little over the top, as if Herb might have had some personal experience along these lines. Keith decided not to ask about it.

They drove on in mildly awkward silence for another minute. There truly was hardly anyone on the road for a weekday afternoon. Keith noticed that of those cars still on the road, nobody was using the slow lane. The Prius' speedometer was hovering around 75 mph, and Keith calculated that everyone still on the freeway was probably guilty of hefty speeding violations. Keith sensed the chilly wind outside the cab with his mind and suddenly felt foolish for thinking his telekinesis was going to be any help to him in unraveling this mystery.

"Wait ... hold on, yup, well I'll be damned. Yer in luck, my friend. 'Ask and ye shall receive,' I guess," Herb said with a sigh to Keith, eyeing a small green car in the distance. "That right there up ahead is a genuine scaredy-fuck, if you'll excuse my French."

Keith sat up and examined the little car in the distance that they were fast approaching. Herb's power of perception was astonishing.

"How can you tell from here?" asked Keith, wondering if the fact that the car was in the far-right lane was the giveaway.

"Oh, just look at how he swerves and darts about," was the contemptuous response. "The goddam fool obviously is shitting a brick and knows he shouldn't be behind the wheel. Why can't they just stay the fuck home?!" Herb was getting a little too emotional on this subject, and once again Keith wondered if Herb hadn't already been involved in some kind of accident with one of these "scaredy-fucks."

"Now, we're going to go zipping by him, and we gonna hope he doesn't flip out. He's three lanes over, so we should be fine, even if he freaks." The worry in Herb's voice was unmistakable.

Keith watched intently, hoping to pick up on some small detail. As they neared the car, a green Honda Civic, Keith felt a whisper of something brush across his awareness. It was like a distant shadow of that strange electric shock he got when he had seized Rupert's floating ball.

The green car made a tiny correction in its steering and Keith felt as if the movement of the car was exposing the thoughts of the driver—thoughts which, according to the Honda's jerky movement, were loaded with apprehension.

Keith's musings were interrupted by Herb's strained voice. "Almost past, we should be good." Their Toyota was now parallel to the green car, and Herb obviously was trying to pay as little attention to the car as possible, keeping his eyes focused on the road ahead of him. Keith wondered about Herb's opinion of these dangerous menaces as he turned back toward the green car.

Keith felt a tiny zap of that strange electricity, stronger than last time, yet still many orders of magnitude less than the mind-consuming shock he had felt with Rupert. This spark came mainly from the green car, but at the same time Keith registered an even tinier, barely perceptible spark coming from Herb. Immediately, the green car slammed on its brakes and swerved a little, but then quickly regained composure.

"See!?!" said Herb, obviously unaware of any exchange taking place. "Did you see the crazy fuck!? And you damn well know that was because of us, there ain't no one else on the road, but you saw: I couldn't have gone any straighter! Mother-fucker should get off the goddam road if he can't handle being passed by a car four freaking lanes away!" Herb's tirade turned into a grumble and trailed off as he caught Keith's wide-eyed stare from the back seat.

Realizing he was gawking, Keith grunted an agreement and turned his eyes back towards the green Honda, now quickly fading in the distance as Herb resumed his cruising speed. All Keith was sure of now was that Rupert was right. Goddam right, in fact. In Keith's mind, there was no doubt the two drivers had just fondled each other's balls. Yet, with the absence of anyone using telekinesis, where was this electricity coming from? And which driver was responsible for the little Honda's swerve?

This finally felt like progress to Keith. He had spent most of the days since his humbling encounter with Rupert trying to figure out the bum's riddles. Now this was something; the Freeway Fear had to be some kind of symptom of ball-fondling in the general public.

The Uber reached its destination without further incident, and without further discussion. Herb's friendly mood had soured since the incident with the green Honda, and his monosyllabic responses to Keith's questions made it clear he was done being chatty. Keith almost felt like Herb was blaming him for their little encounter. After getting out and watching Herb peel off, Keith checked his phone and saw his small trip cost over a hundred dollars. Supply and demand, Keith supposed.

Keith's destination was Mercer Slough Nature Park in Bellevue, a wooded park seldom visited by locals, although the paths were well-kept. Accompanied by overcast but unseasonably warm weather, Keith zipped his hoodie and began walking down one of the wood-chip paths toward the center of the park, lost in thought.

It was obvious that the emergence of Teks was not everything that was going on in the world. Though Keith had discovered his own power before the mainstream media even acknowledged anything unusual was happening, he knew that his power was just another symptom, not the cause, of whatever it was that was going on. Telekinesis did not account for the bizarre news that seemed to get weirder every day, and it certainly could not account for the Freeway Fear. Keith wondered what he would have done if the ride had gone awry. Would he have really been able to catch Herb's Prius in mid-flip with his mind? And what about the green Honda? Was he morally responsible for trying to catch that car as well? The question of responsibility made Keith uneasy.

Keith neared what he thought was the middle of the park and ventured off the path into the woods. He hadn't seen another soul since he arrived, but just to be sure, he paused and double checked that nobody was following him.

Nobody watching but the birds.

Keith checked the latest headlines on his phone. Sharks on Florida beaches. Big ones. Never mind Teks and the Freeway Fear, there were also monsters and miracles. Keith pondered what possible relation these things could have with each other.

Keith stopped and scratched his head, unable to arrive at any conclusions, but was pleased that he had so many new questions to think about.

Keith cleared his mind, looked around, and concentrated on the new task at hand. He looked up at the tall trees around him and grinned widely, finally allowing himself to be giddy with excitement over this moment. This was an experiment waiting at the back of his mind ever since that first evening in the bathtub, but only recently had he gained the mental power and the courage to attempt it.

Keith decided he would remember this as Test Flight #1, and held out his hands, steadying himself for takeoff.

3 Days

Thomas Bonner sat on his porch, smoked his cigar, and watched the little traffic that passed by his farm.

After the events of the Moondog Festival had been distributed and embellished by the Greenfield Gossip Grapevine, just about the whole town was terrorized into seclusion. As spread out as Greenfield's population already was, seclusion wasn't that unusual in the first place.

At any rate, Tom had trouble even caring about the rest of the town because of the miracle going on in his own home.

Tom and Judy were both aware that her unbelievable cooking skill had no earthly explanation. The Bonners were officially being *Touched By the Weird*, but at least it was a tasty kind of weird. Even though the source of Judy's powers of cooking was mysterious, the news made it clear that they were not unique.

Tom had a lot of mixed emotions about this. On the one hand, it was a tad unnerving to have their lives affected so personally by the worldwide phenomenon. On the other hand, Judy was a superhero.

Watching Judy cook, Tom had found himself wishing that he had some new power as well. So far, though, Tom was just as ordinary as he had ever been, as far as he could tell. His attempts to cook were as clumsy and futile as ever, and the few farming chores he had tried seemed just as difficult as he remembered. Admittedly, though, he hadn't started any serious farm work. He needed a working tractor for that.

Tom had retrieved his hopeless JD from an abandoned Henry's Auto Repair a few days ago. The damn thing still wouldn't start, though at this point Tom figured even Greg-the-Mechanic probably should be given a break. Maybe whatever made Judy a good cook also made little Greg a terrible mechanic. There definitely wasn't anything in the headlines about stubborn tractors.

The sound of a car coming down the road in the distance interrupted Tom's train of thought.

The only time that Tom ever felt touched by all the weirdness was that day at the Moondog festival, when Danny had asked him if he had known where the pea pod was. Never mind that every kid in the contest did, too, Tom suspected maybe his power would be foretelling the future.

So instead of leaning his rocker forward to see who was coming like he usually did, Tom leaned back, closed his eyes, and attempted to foretell who was coming down the road.

Tom knew he had to predict quickly, since the approaching auto was often in full view before he could decide what he was predicting. He thought about turning his chair around so he couldn't see down the road, but quickly decided against that. To anyone driving by, Tom sitting backwards on his porch would only add to the eerie ambiance of the times.

The Freeway Fear, which was all anyone from bigger towns like Bisby could talk about, was of little concern to Greenfield. Those who regularly drove the two-lane roads that made up the countryside weren't reporting anything too unusual, aside from a certain lack of people "out n' about" these days. The town remained small over the years because no freeway ever found a reason to come within 50 miles of city limits.

As the vehicle approached, Tom blew an exasperated sigh. Tom recognized the sound of Carlos' truck immediately. He was not having much luck predicting anything. Maybe being a fortune teller wasn't his thing either.

Rather than continuing down the road as usual, Carlos the Mexican's muddy blue Chevy turned in and drove up to the Bonner residence.

Happy for the visit, Tom waited for Carlos' engine to stop. "Hey Carlos! What's shakin?"

Carlos jumped out and smiled a strained smile at Tom before striding over to the chair next to Tom and hurriedly sitting down. This was very unusual behavior for Carlos, who usually greeted Tom, shook hands, and had assessed the beer situation before settling into his seat.

"Hay Tom." Carlos sounded sad.

"Well, what's up, Carlos? Why so glum? We got beer," Tom turned his head to call out to Judy, "Pumpkin? Can you get our guest a beer?"

Tom turned a concerned face back to Carlos, whose foot anxiously bounced up and down. Carlos clearly had something on his mind. Hopefully a beer would help.

"I kint stind it, mayn!" Carlos' accent seemed especially thick today. Normally it was barely detectible, but today it sounded like Carlos had just stepped off the boat, so to speak.

Carlos could see Tom's surprise, which only distressed him further. He pointed an accusing finger at Tom. "See! See! Ya kin hear es! E kint talk no more!"

Carlos was obviously very upset, and Tom was shocked beyond words. Yes, Carlos was Mexican, but Carlos had lived in Illinois for many years, and his English was nothing but fluent. Tom had never had a hard time understanding him, but now it was as if he had forgotten even the most basic pronunciation.

Carlos chattered a string of words at Tom that was probably English, but Tom could only pick up something about a store and people staring.

Tom was at a loss. "You're not funnin' with me?"

The expression on Carlos's face was no joke. The poor man looked like he was holding back tears.

"Hey, Carlos." Judy's voice came from the doorway behind them. She was standing with two beers and a look of concern.

Carlos took one look at Judy's face and knew she had overheard his bungling attempt to speak English. He stood and turned away in shame, swearing in Spanish, and started walking back to his truck.

Tom opened his mouth to call after his distressed friend, but found himself speechless. What could he say?

Carlos quickly drove away leaving the Bonners stunned and staring at each other on the porch. This was a whole new level of weirdness.

After discussing how maybe not all new powers were good things while eating Judy's exquisite beef wellington, Tom and Judy went to bed.

In the middle of the night, there was a very faint noise outside. It wasn't loud enough to wake either of the Bonners, but if they had been awake, they would have heard what sounded like wolves howling in the distance, coming from the direction of Edgar's farm.

2 Days

Cory Nelson hopped on the bus heading home from school feeling the repressed giddiness shared by the entire school body. School was out. Maybe forever. Probably not forever, but a kid could dream.

Cory found an open seat in his usual mid-bus location. He wasn't cool enough for the back, yet also wasn't picked on enough to need the protection of the front of the bus. Securing his backpack next to him, Cory couldn't help but overhear Suzie's jabbering with the girl behind her. Back to her full Suzie form, her mouth was a blur of semi-important news.

"..and I heard from Jamie that his school closed yesterday. But he said his friend's school wasn't closing until the end of the week. But I hear they're all closing. No more school! Yay!" Suzie paused to take a breath.

"Yay!" squealed the girl behind Suzie, with her spectacled eyes locked on Suzie's performance. Suzie continued.

"You know why, right? You know why there's no more school? Why we get to go home?" Suzie prodded.

"Teks?" ventured the girl.

"Monsters!" shouted Suzie.

"Monsters! No!" shrieked the girl.

"Yes! Monsters are real and coming for you! You better believe it! Watch out! They'll get you!" Suzie partially collapsed laughing along with the girl.

Monsters? That's dumb, thought Cory. Although he hadn't been a fan of the dark when he was younger, only preschoolers believed in monsters. Cory was sure it was because of the Teks. He didn't think monsters were real, but magic sure was! Cory wished he could become a Tek. The things he would do!

To Cory's dismay, Jeff Hammond, bully extraordinaire, arrived out of nowhere, grabbed Cory's backpack, and tossed it to the back of the bus.

"Hey!" was Cory's reflexive response as we watched his backpack soar over the seats and crash to the floor in the isle near the back of the bus. Jeff then slammed his giant ogre of a body right next to Cory, pinning him next to the window. Cory wasn't sure where Jeff's backpack was. Sometimes he wondered if Jeff even owned one.

"Hey Squeaker," the ogre grunted.

Cory's face began to turn red as frustration set in. He was trapped. He wanted to go get his bag off the dirty floor, but he wasn't getting past lard-ass, so that meant either bounding over one of the seats like a coward or just waiting until Jeff left. Cory wondered what Jeff wanted. Jeff had never sat next to him before; it made it look too much like they were actual friends.

"What do you want, Jeff?" Cory said. Cory was pleased with how this came out. It felt very grown-up and properly hid his fear.

Jeff's response was automatic. He turned and punched Cory in the arm.

"Ow," Cory whimpered. He knew if he said anything else, he'd probably get punched again.

Jeff looked frustrated.

"See! Did you see that, Squeaks!? I didn't do it! I didn't!" Jeff said.

"Yes, you did!" Cory said, eyes teary. Jeff wasn't making any sense, but there was no way Jeff was going to make Cory say he hadn't just punched him.

"No, you don't get it! I'm not like that. Well, maybe sometimes, but not all the time. But today I can't *not* do it! I fuckin shoved Mike into the wall for no reason and I even fuckin *like* Mike!" Jeff said.

Cory sighed an experienced sigh. Whatever Jeff was talking about, if he actually tried to understand it, it would only reveal some new dumb game that Jeff invented. Cory didn't buy this "uncontrollable bullying" crap for one second.

"Whatever, Jeff, how about you go 'not do it' somewhere else?" said Cory as he glanced back at his backpack. Cory was proud of this zinger as well.

"God! Will you just stop squeaking for just one second?!" Jeff said, acting all fed-up with Cory. As he said this, Jeff got up and moved to a different seat by himself, shaking his head.

Immediately Cory bounded up and snatched his backpack from the floor and repositioned it to defend against intruders, this time keeping his arm through the strap, even though it was tender from where Jeff had hit it. Since school was closing, with any luck, this could be the last bus ride he would have to take with that asshole Jeff Hammond.

1 Day

Keith Pennison turned off his phone and put it in pocket. He was at The Drip again, this time the lone customer. He was out of coffee, and he was done watching YouTube.

He had just finished watching the "SWAT TPK" video. This particular viral clip already had close to five million views and showed an entire SWAT team attempting to shoot a single chubby Latino Tek and getting slaughtered in the process. The news reported that the Tek in the video was later killed by another Tek. Keith wondered what that had looked like.

Keith tossed his cup in the trash and began walking back to his apartment. It was a drizzly Seattle spring afternoon, the kind that required a jacket but not quite a raincoat. Excellent hoodie weather.

Keith kept trying to scan the outrageous stories in his hand while not falling on his face. His news feed kept telling him the same thing: Things were getting out of hand.

Teks were popping up everywhere. Keith originally assumed his was a rare power which needed to be kept hidden from prying scientists, but the more YouTube videos he had watched, the more it seemed like the scientists would have no shortage of test subjects. Nor would the test subjects be doing anything they didn't want to do.

The government was also sort of freaking out. At first, there was supposed to be a voluntary registry where Teks could register themselves for some vague patriotic purpose. Registering Teks sounded like a terrible idea, and probably others thought the same, considering the news seemed to have stopped mentioning it.

Keith's mind swam as he was noisily passed by a line of cars and swiped up to the next story.

Internationally, several countries had erupted into civil wars of some form or another. Oppressive regimes that ruled with an iron fist for decades suddenly found their headquarters leveled by angry Teks with grudges. Keith was glad that at least in the US, Teks didn't seem to think their government needed attacking.

A screech of tires snapped Keith's head up from his phone and he turned around to see a Loomis armored truck screeching to a stop with its wheels locked. At first glance, it looked like the driver had just slammed on the brakes, but the way the tires slid sideways betrayed unnatural movement of the truck.

A small, skinny woman approached the truck. She was young, maybe mid-twenties, wearing a puffy silver jacket and sporting wild hair with a purple streak in it. Her hands were outstretched in front of her, with her purple painted nails clawing at the air. Her grin was malicious.

Behind the truck, car doors opened and people fled, apparently as familiar with this scene as Keith was. Armored trucks were not safe anymore.

The back wall of the truck began to twist impossibly, the steel emitting a screeching punctuated by the occasional crack of glass.

Keith tried to casually close on the truck as people fled past him. The girl Tek advanced on the truck as the metal twisted and tore off in pieces. The strength of her power was impressive, but the way she clawed at the air with her hands while she was using it was puzzling. Keith didn't need to move his hands when using his power, so why would she?

Keith's heart raced but couldn't find a reason to act yet.

The passenger of the truck opened the door and ran, his pudgy face pale with fear as he slipped on the slick road.

The driver was not as easily scared and jumped out of the truck with a shotgun drawn, planted his feet and pointed it at the Tek's head.

"Back off!" shouted the driver at the girl.

Mostly torn open by now, the truck stopped shrieking as the girl lowered her arms and turned towards the driver. Keith inched closer.

"If you fire that shit at me, you're fucking dead, bro." There was hot anger in her voice. This girl was not going to being told what to do.

"Just keep your hands down and walk away," was the man's response, obviously not grasping the power dynamic. "Back off and nobody gets hurt."

The girl slowly raised one of her hands, her fingers still grasping the air.

The man, trained to deal with firearms, didn't hesitate and fired quickly three times, the shotgun blasts echoing off the buildings. Each shot was accompanied by the sound of a ricochet, the last one hitting the ground right next to where Keith was standing. Unlike the girl who was ready for it, Keith realized with horror that he had almost just been ended by a stray bullet.

"Your funeral," the girl said, repositioning and bringing her hands out in front of her again as the guard lowered his gun with his mouth open in disbelief.

She was going to tear him in half. Keith had to act and did the first thing that came to mind.

"No," stated Keith, reaching out with his mind, reflexively accompanied by his hand, and locking the figure of the guard in its place.

The girl's consciousness invaded Keith's. There was so much hurt, and this man needed to pay for it. Keith could feel the edges of his invisible cage begin to peel away from the guard.

"No," thought Keith. Ripping open another human being was unconscionable in any circumstance. The peeling stopped. The girl's angry face turned towards Keith.

"Really?" she asked incredulously.

The girl's thoughts and feelings vanished as she dropped her arms. Keith released the man with the shotgun who fell to the floor, gasping for air.

"Fine, but I'm taking this and you're not stopping me," she declared, striding up to the torn open truck, giving it one last ripping gesture, and snatching a heavy white bag.

Keith couldn't find any objection to that. Never mind that money was not worth fighting about, he wasn't sure he could stop her if he wanted to.

Released from his paralysis and having partially regained his composure, the man with the shotgun gawked back and forth between Keith and the gun.

"You," said Keith to the guard. "Don't try to shoot Teks. Someone could get killed." Like an innocent bystander.

Keith turned to see where the girl was going but she was nowhere to be seen. All that remained was the vague feeling of her mind. She had pulled a Rupert. Keith turned and noticed that a crowd had gathered, fearfully watching his every move.

Suddenly embarrassed by the attention, Keith turned and tried to nonchalantly continue his walk. Still unsure of how to get people to ignore him, he hoped the scene was scary enough to discourage anyone from following him. After walking a few minutes, Keith glanced behind him and didn't see anyone. Even so, his heart still raced. The whole encounter was a sharp reminder that he was not invincible and needed some sort of always-on defense against bullets. The internet had plenty of videos of Teks getting caught unaware by a bullet they didn't see coming.

Keith checked his phone again and saw a fresh batch of sensational stories. Mental hospitals and prisons all over the country were having a hard time with angry Teks. It seemed the whole idea of "justice" was starting to unravel. Keith hoped he would end up on the right side of things.

4 Hours

Having put Cory to bed an hour earlier, Adam and Claire Nelson had drifted off to sleep on the couch with the TV on. They had been glued to it all day long, hearing one fantastic thing after another.

3 Hours

"Lights out" was over an hour ago at the Westvale Federal penitentiary, and Jacob was on his top bunk staring at the ceiling, having more trouble falling asleep than usual. Teks were everywhere. The government had lost control. The possibilities were endless. It was only a matter of time.

2 HOURS

Tom and Judy had both been asleep less than an hour before they were woken up with a start. There was a noise coming from outside. It was howling. It was loud.

It lasted a good long minute, and it was by far the scariest sound Tom had ever heard. Unmistakably, it was the long, mournful howl of wolves in the distance, but also unnaturally echoic. Tom made a conscious effort to avoid picturing what was making the sounds.

Tom crept out of bed and unearthed his shotgun from the closet, crawling back into bed after lying it on his nightstand. The sounds came from the direction of Edgar's farm, and even though neighborly concern made him want to check on Edgar, the unearthly characteristic of the howling overrode any thoughts he had of being brave.

Aside from the growing number of reports of people with superpowers, there were also stories in the news about monsters. To put it bluntly, monsters were real, and monsters could kill. There was no way Tom was venturing off in the middle of the night chasing monsters. Tom hoped Edgar could hold his own.

The Bonners did not hear the wolves again that night and eventually drifted back to sleep.

1 Hour

Keith Pennison had tried to stay awake for the big event. "Meet a Tek" they were calling it. Some powerful Tek was going to do a live demonstration from the Universal Studios lot and then do an interview with the late-night host Johnny Stevens.

But the encounter with the scary girl Tek and the truck had taken a lot out of him. Thrilled to have saved a life, yet also terrified that he had risked his own, Keith was exhausted from replaying the incident in his mind all day.

Keith fell asleep on his bed with his phone in his hand.

David Archer was not the first person recruited to perform the special demonstration. Two other people possessing the ability were scheduled to demonstrate, but twice during the day the producers found someone dramatically better at telekinesis than the previously scheduled guest. David Archer was by far the best qualified, as the mass of objects did not seem to affect his ability to control them. Best of all, from the producers' point of view, he had a calm, collected air and an attractive appearance, ideal for the demonstration. The producers sought someone who would not scare the audience, which was expected to be in record numbers after ads touting the demonstration had played all day.

David Archer was a thin, young man in his late twenties who seemed genuinely in control and unworried about his abilities, as opposed to most of the other known Teks, who tended to be slightly alarmed about their own newfound powers.

The demonstration itself was not an earth-shattering event. People had been watching Teks display their power on the internet for the past few days, and this was just another, higher production-value version of the common demonstrations.

The demonstration went like this:

A long table was brought out with an assortment of items on it, and next to it was a shiny new Tesla EV. There were four white softballs, four black bowling balls, and ten long, shiny steel blades about an inch in width and 5 feet in length. All the objects were chosen by the producers, except the blades, which were requested by Archer, promising to do very visually stunning things with them. A quick demonstration convinced the producers to allow it, although they made sure the blades were dull. Trusting a Tek, especially one with David's impressive talent, was a given. If a Tek turned violent, everyone knew that the only way to stop them was another Tek.

The demonstration began with David Archer calmly walking onto the stage to applause, sardonically nodding to the lone soldier stationed at the side of the stage. Requiring an armed guard at Tek demonstrations was a controversial rule, both for its rude implications and for its complete uselessness.

Archer then turned and looked at the table. All four softballs levitated and began spinning in a circular motion above and in front of David. David kept his hands behind his back, an expression of mild concentration on his face, both of which were unusual for Teks at the time. The audience applauded politely.

David slowly drew his eyes down from the circling softballs, and then the four bowling balls lifted from the table and began circling as well. The circling bowling balls joined the circling softballs in interlocking rings, a fantastic figure eight. The effortless expression on David's face brought cheers from the audience. Heavy items such as bowling balls were known to be more difficult for Teks to move.

The producers expected David to lift the blades next, as he had done in rehearsal, and save the Tesla stunt for last. David instead ignored the blades on the table and slowly turned his eye to the car, which lifted off the ground and hovered gently into position above the two circling rings of balls, thirty feet in the air. In a display of control, David expanded the circling rings and pulled the car down to the middle, where he spun it vertically. The crowd loved every minute of it.

David then reached his hand up for dramatic effect and stopped every floating object in its place, hanging motionless above his head. He then guided all the objects back to their place on the table and the Tesla to the floor at once.

Next, he looked at the blades, which rose vertically, stacked neatly one on top of each other. Instead of the spinning, theatrical display the producers had been shown earlier, David maneuvered the stack of blades to float vertically in front of him, still stacked together.

David casually turned to the Army guard standing at the edge of the stage. Shocked gasps rippled through the crowd as the guard's M-16 flew from his shoulder and came to float about 5 feet in front of David, barrel pointing directly at David's face. Between David and the gun was the stack of floating knives, which David then spun in front of him like a fan at an incredible speed. Next came an ear-shattering volley of automatic rifle fire, apparently shooting directly at David, who had only the 10 spinning blades as protection.

The smoking machine gun, clip emptied, flew back and wrapped around the embarrassed soldier's shoulder. It was clear the soldier had been ordered to take no action.

David then stopped the blades from spinning and spread them out in front of him, showing the audience all the stopped bullets stuck in the blades. The audience erupted in applause.

If that was where the show had ended, then probably nothing special would have happened that night. However, after the demonstration, Johnny Stevens brought David Archer to his interviewing desk to chat about his abilities. After about 10 minutes of conversation and jokes, in which the host demonstrated his own talent of transforming his spooked audience into a chuckling upbeat crowd, David Archer interrupted one of the host's questions.

"Hang on a minute, Johnny," David said.

"Okay," agreed the host.

"I have a secret to tell you," David said with a wry smile.

"I'm excellent at keeping secrets on national television," the host cavorted to the delight of the audience. "By all means, do tell us, uh I mean me, your secret!"

David then leaned forward, the host leaned forward, and David Archer whispered very quietly into his ear, "Everyone can do it."

Though David knew the words he spoke were true, he expected everyone else in the world to start moving small objects just as he had done, slowly losing their beliefs in physics and gaining skill with their ability.

However, that is not what happened.

Immediately after David's whisper, when Johnny Stevens jumped back from Mr. Archer and shouted incredulously at the top of his lungs, "Everyone can do it!?," the host believed in his heart that this statement was true. When the studio audience heard it, they believed it too. Minutes later, after millions of viewers heard those same words and watched the studio audience descend into chaos, they believed it as well.

The time of the broadcast was 1:31 a.m. Eastern Standard Time. For most people, that was the moment that reality cracked.

1 Minute

Roy watched the spinning roulette ball make its rounds before its inevitable plunge towards finality. He was feeling good and had bet fifty on this drop, yet now he was questioning his decision. Naturally, there was nothing he could do about it at this point. The commitment was made, the choice chosen. All that was left was the blissful agony as hope and fear spun their terrifying dance before lady luck made her ultimate judgement. Part of the fun was that there was no turning back. Roy sometimes wished he liked some other game.

Round and round. It was a Friday night in Vegas, and Roy had expected the casino to be more hopping. Their room was at the Golden Nugget casino in "Old Vegas," where one's odds were substantially better than at the newer, fancier casinos on the strip. That was the agreed upon logic with which Roy and his wife had chosen the Golden Nugget. The unspoken reason was that off-strip casinos were a hell of a lot cheaper.

Roy sucked on the straw of his nearly empty drink and checked his watch. He had been on the roulette table for the greater portion of the night. It was getting late, and he knew his wife was waiting for him in the hotel room, though he hoped she had gone to sleep already. Somehow, in ways that were foreign to Roy, gambling seemed to tire his wife.

10:30. He should probably head back before 11:00. He wondered if the cocktail waitress would pass by in time for him to squeeze in one more drink.

Round and round the ball went. Roy always thought they must use magnets or something to make the balls spin so long before dropping.

There were two other players at the table. One was an older Asian man who somehow was sweating despite the air conditioning, and the other was a frail, even older lady with wispy, white hair whose eyes were hidden behind thickly layered glasses. None of them had been very lucky that evening, and they all wore the same blank expression, hiding their frustration. The dealer was also not working very hard for his tip. He was a middle-aged man going through the motions, his mind and his eyes conspicuously elsewhere.

The time was 10:31 pm Pacific.

As Roy watched, the ball slowed down and stopped. It didn't drop, it just stopped in mid-spin, hanging impossibly above the circling numbers. The Asian man thought the ball should head to 23 red. The old lady thought it should head to 31 black. The dealer thought it should have kept spinning for 6 more seconds. Roy couldn't understand how he suddenly knew all these things.

A massive crash came from the slots behind the players, startling them out of their daze. A slot machine had erupted in screws, gears, plates, and coins, spewing its guts behind them on the floor.

Chaos erupted in all directions around Roy. One of the card tables next to him flipped over, knocking over the dealer, and three more slot machines exploded behind him. Roy instinctively grabbed the table in front of him as he was jostled by gamblers jumping up and grabbing cash. Women everywhere started screaming. Roy thought of his wife.

People immediately started running in all directions. Shocked, but struggling to keep his head together, Roy frantically shoveled most of his chips into his jacket. The Asian man was gone, having abandoned his small pile of chips, and the old lady still sat rigid on her stool, eyes hidden, mouth hung open.

Some loud sounds of metal twisting and bending were coming from the rows of slot machines as the mob panicked and started rushing for the door. Roy jumped off his chair and was hit in the shoulder by something. Spinning around but keeping his feet, his assailant was nowhere to be seen. It was as if the air had just shoulder-checked him.

The entire wall of the cashier's cage ripped open and fell to the ground. Wide-eyed cashiers stared in horror at the empty space where their barrier once existed, perched comically on their stools, unable to comprehend the sudden view of madness that had engulfed the entire casino floor.

Cash was everywhere. Bills floated down like snow as odd clumps of the stuff flew purposefully through the air above Roy's head. Roy slipped on some bills as he clambered with the rest of the crowd towards the door. People didn't know whether to grab cash with glee or run screaming with terror. Most managed to do a little bit of both.

Roy couldn't resist and stopped to grab a handful of twenties in the midst of the chaos. Stuffing them into his jacket, and about to go back for another handful, Roy spotted a bill with blood on it. That settled it. Roy turned and used both arms to run full speed towards the door.

The panicked horde spewed forth from the casino into the street like a river, with Roy shoulder-to-shoulder among his fellow gamblers. As he stumbled out onto the strip, the ambient noise changed from loud, close screams, to a sickly roar of many, many distant screams.

Outside the casino, the famous Fremont Street Experience, an artificial canopy of millions of lights, was in the grip of a nasty transformation. The pulsing, twinkling ceiling was twisting and wrenching like a dishrag, emitting an awful grinding noise as a shower of glass from broken light bulbs rained onto the crowd below.

As soon as he escaped the river of terrified gamblers pouring out of the casino, Roy crawled into a corner near a group of people wearing shocked, blank expressions. Roy felt he would belong with this group.

There began another very loud and unfamiliar rumbling noise that shook the ground. Roy didn't want to know what this was, but begrudgingly looked up with glazed eyes to see that the hotel building next to his was in the process of toppling over. The rumbling was coming from the imploding base of the hotel, where a cloud of debris was rushing towards him at breakneck speed.

More disturbing was the fact that the hotel was toppling in his direction.

"Shit," stated Roy. This was Roy's last word.

1 Minute

Seth adjusted his seatbelt on Delta flight 343 with service to Dallas as the noise of the landing gear rumbled its retraction into the belly of the plane. He couldn't seem to get comfortable, either with the way his middle seat constrained his waist, or with the fact that he was hurtling through the air on a flimsy aluminum tube full of people who, like him, just *might* be Teks.

The time was 12:31am Central.

Suddenly, Seth realized something was different. While moving anything with his power took great concentration before, the back of the chair in front of him suddenly felt like it could be ripped off its hinges if he so willed it.

The cabin was instantly filled with sounds of chair backs being ripped off their hinges. Screams followed as Seth tried to make sense of what was about to happen. The plane lurched as pieces of aluminum and chair cushion fell to the ground before being flung into the roof by g-forces.

Seth knew what was about to happen. He had been imagining it since he boarded. He grabbed the air around him to protect himself from the maelstrom of metal engulfing the flight.

The side of the plane tore open, sucking the air along with several passengers outside. The force of the wind immediately exploded the contents of the plane as if someone had pulled a confetti popper. Pieces of plane, seats, people, pieces of people, anything and everything went everywhere as Seth closed his eyes and held himself together until he heard nothing but wind.

Seth opened his eyes to find himself hurtling towards the ground, chair-first, still strapped in, while debris and other passengers plummeted next to him. He knew he had only seconds to act before impact, so he grabbed his chair with all his Tek might and pulled up. Surprisingly, the air slowed, his descent calmed, and the debris that had been surrounding him accelerated away from him. A large chunk of metal hit Seth's air shield above him and spun harmlessly away, as Seth was again shocked by the sudden strength and ease of his Tek powers.

Seth looked around, unsure of whether he was still descending, considering his height, and saw several other passengers floating down like him, also still strapped into their seats.

Everything had happened so fast. It was suddenly quiet. And cold. He counted around five other passengers that appeared to have been spared. Looking down, he caught sight of a few more. Seth couldn't see where the plane hit the ground, but also failed to see the fireball he was expecting. Seth wondered how many people on that plane had just died. Then he wondered how many planes had just crashed. Then he wondered exactly how the rest of the world was faring.

1 Minute

Lucy Solberg calmly surveyed the patients in front of her. Everyone secretly knows what their own physical perfection means, Lucy mused, as she repeatedly mulled over her plan in her head.

It was nighttime at the St. Regis hospital, located just outside Portland, Oregon, and things were relatively quiet, at least in the ER. Lucy stood in front of a row of five patients, each hooked up to various machines and tubes, all blinking and whirring with soft rhythm as the patients slumbered. Another row of patients lay behind her, and occasionally Paul would walk through, checking the machines and glancing at the softly glowing screens.

Lucy looked out of place in the hospital, with her long black hair and custom-fitted blue jumpsuit. Not even twenty years old yet, she had a sharp, striking beauty about her that was attractive by almost any standard. Paul, a young orderly, walked up to her and navigated around her, all without looking up from the chart he was carrying.

Lucy preferred to be unseen.

She knew the orderly's name was Paul because up until a few weeks ago, Lucy was employed as a nurse at St. Regis, although her last day wasn't exactly clear. After watching Dr. Parker perform one of his first magic surgeries, she was confident she wasn't needed there anymore.

Dr. Parker, according to the rest of the nurses, was the lord savior Jesus Christ. He was able to single-handedly resolve any trauma case that came through the door. Lucy had watched him perform entire operations by himself in a matter of seconds. The scalpel flew through the patient's flesh, followed immediately by the airborne suture. Suction obeyed Dr. Parker's every glance, but it was hardly needed because the patient was sewn up in an instant before even having a chance to bleed.

Doctor Freaking Parker, Lucy thought to herself. Lucy closed her eyes and suppressed her distaste for him, which was at least somewhat due to her general feeling of disgust towards doctors. Naturally, Dr. Parker accepted the role of the savior. What an ass. She was going to enjoy putting him out of a job.

It was 10:31 p.m.

About ten feet from Lucy, Paul dropped his hands down from his chart, but the chart stayed in place, as if suspended by a magician's wire. Paul's confused "what the-" was cut off by Mr. Highgrove's sudden thrashing as his intubation tube was launched from his throat by an unknown force.

"Oh shit," whispered Lucy.

Paul's chart crashed to the floor, startling Paul, pulling his attention away from Mr. Highgrove, all while the rest of the ER patients begin stirring and ejecting the various machines and needles plugged into their bodies.

Someone's bed fell over. A scream and a crash echoed from the hallway.

"Everyone can do it." These words were clear. This was now a fact. There was more there that made less sense. Something about a Tesla? Lucy didn't have time for that.

"I guess it's now or never," sighed Lucy.

Lucy crouched down and moved her arms and hands as if she were grasping a volleyball tightly near her chest. Her face fixed into an expression of serene concentration, as if she was straining to hear soft music.

Paul the orderly stood rooted to the ground, watching the scene unfold with wide eyes and an open mouth, wholly unsure of what to believe. Mr. Highgrove was gasping for air on the floor, miraculously able to gasp, yet not miraculously enough to breathe normally. Several of the other patients were also on the floor in various states of distress, and loose drip liquids mixed with blood splattered everywhere. The sudden appearance of nurse Lucy in a crouched position, dressed like she was going clubbing, was simply one more thing that didn't make sense, although he wasn't sure if he just didn't notice her there before.

A thin but piercing white bolt of electricity sparked across Lucy's fingertips. This was quickly followed by another, then more, as unknown energy gathered towards her clutched hands. White lightning danced across her trembling fingers until, after a few seconds, a solid ball of hot white electricity had formed inside her loose-fingered grasp.

Lucy then tightly wrapped her body over the lightning ball, which quickly grew, passing through and enveloping her body.

Paul took a step back.

The opaque ball of white lightning kept expanding, and Lucy kept concentrating, locked in a crouching fetal position, with one hand over the other fist.

The first person, other than Lucy, to be touched by this white electricity was a lung cancer patient named Joe Orson in a bed directly behind her. Rudely awoken, but numb to the sounds of this life and resigned to being chained to his bed by a breathing tube, Mr. Orson did not move when the noise started. But when the current touched the top of his scalp, it jolted through his body in a violent spasm that left Mr. Orson on the floor on all fours, coughing for breath.

Seconds later the lightning rocketed through Mr. Orson's two neighbors, who also had little time to be afraid. They both spasmed out of their beds with arcs of white voltage flowing through their bodies.

The sphere kept expanding through walls, ceilings, and floors. The patients who were mobile tried to run from it, but there was nowhere to go, as the windows of the fifth floor did not open. One by one, the lightning caught everyone.

Mr. Olson looked up at the bed that had been his home for most of the last year. He then looked at the ventilator that had been keeping him alive and stared at the nozzle that he had violently ejected from his esophagus moments earlier.

The screams of people desperately trying to escape the relentless sphere of lightning did not bother Mr. Olson as he effortlessly stood up tall, using bulging muscles in his legs that only moments earlier had been atrophied beyond any hope of recovery.

Mr. Olson looked to his left and saw Mrs. Kinshaw sitting on the floor, wearing a shocked expression of happiness that Mr. Olsen knew meant the constant pain of her advanced stage cervical cancer no longer bothered her.

Mr. Olsen took a deep breath with lungs that felt stronger to him than they had back before he had taken his first puff on his very first cigarette. Through his crusty beard and using vocal chords undamaged by either a lifetime of smoking or by his plastic breathing tube, Mr. Olsen let out a bellowing laugh of triumphant exhilaration that echoed down the halls.

The lightning touched everyone at St. Regis hospital that day. There was no escaping it. And wherever the lightning touched, people were healed.

Diseases vanished, wounds closed, broken limbs mended, and missing limbs grew back, all in the blink of an eye and a convulsion of the body. An old man who was born blind suddenly opened his eyes and was forced to deal with an additional sense. The wheelchair-bound stood up and tangoed. Fake hips and artificial knees were rejected from flesh with ripping force, instantly replaced by the real thing, and leaving no trace of their presence. Those who felt the lightning at St. Regis's hospital that day described the experience as having all their ailments slapped out of them all at once.

Paul crouched against the corner screaming as the wall of lightning advanced upon him, erasing his last escape. Seconds later he stood up and noticed that the carpal tunnel ache in his wrist was gone and he did not have a shred of fatigue from staying up two nights in a row.

Minutes later, massive throngs of rejoicing patients in hospital gowns convinced Paul that his nursing duties were no longer required. Even Dr. Parker's career was probably over, he thought, as Paul officially abandoned his duties and joined the crowd in their jubilant exodus.

At the edge of the hospital grounds, where the euphoric celebration was tapering off, Lucy casually strolled out into the darkness. The new fact of this world, that everyone on the planet was now a Tek, was downright mind-boggling. Yet it still seemed like a secondary concern to this crowd. Lucy couldn't help wearing a sly grin as she sauntered off towards her next destination.

MINUTE 1

Jacob Christenson was awoken by the sound of sinister cackling.

Waking from a deep, dreamless sleep, Jacob cracked open his eyes to the dim light of nighttime at Westvale and stared at the all-too-familiar ceiling.

Prisoners were cackling.

All throughout the cell block, there were giggles, dark chuckles, and the occasional maniacal laugh. At first, Jacob wondered what joke he was missing, but immediately the punchline was clear. The ceiling of his cell, at which he was staring, was giving him a peculiar feeling. Jacob could feel the cold concrete, he could feel through the solid rock, and he could sense the microscopic specks of marker where someone had once written long ago.

It had happened. Jacob had been given some gift, and from the sound of it, so had a lot of other snickering inmates. Jacob tested his guess by seizing on the ceiling above him and seeing if he could shake it. A few pebbles landed on his face in confirmation. A smile crept across his face. The balance of power in the clink had just been flipped on its face.

Metallic creaking sounds began echoing along the cell block, getting louder every second. Jacob leapt down from his bunk and tried to assess the situation. There was a shuddering somewhere deep in the floor, shaking the walls, and the shriek of twisting metal bars was everywhere. Jacob's mind raced, as only one thing was absolutely certain: the Westvale federal penitentiary was about to go completely insane.

Jacob was ready. He had prepared for two possible contingencies: either the powers would trickle down to him, inmate by inmate, in which case he would rely on his cunning and manipulation to survive as order slowly crumbled, or everyone would get the power at the same time, in which case he would have to move smarter and faster than all his recently emancipated enemies.

"Don't move" said Jacob to Darrey, who was sitting in the bottom bunk staring at Jacob with wide eyes.

Jacob reconsidered. "And if you would be so kind, please focus your attention *elsewhere*," Jacob snapped through his teeth. Darrey looked down quickly and then away, trying to look at something other than Jacob. Jacob had to proceed under the assumption that Darrey was not going to be a threat.

Jacob turned his attention back to the bars of his cell as the noise outside turned more violent with the occasional scream and crash. He grabbed the bars with his mind and prepared himself for some sort of effort. He willed the bars to be pulled inward with all his strength. Immediately, it was clear to Jacob how to wield the power. It wasn't concentration or exertion, it was confidence. You didn't ask the bars to move or think about the bars moving; you demanded it. Right now. As someone who spent his life using confidence as a weapon, Jacob swelled with pride and ripped every bar off his cell with ease. There were eight bars in all, and Jacob examined the twisted metal ends of them as they floated around him.

Darrey, incapable of watching anything other than Jacob despite his orders, turned wide eyes towards the opening that previously had bars on it. Darrey knew to wait for Jacob's move.

Above the rising ruckus, Jacob detected a familiar grunt and wheeze coming from down the hallway.

Jacob readied his grasp on the eight floating metal bars as he lined them up parallel to the floor in front of him, all pointed at the doorway. He had expected Alberto to reach his cell first, but it sounded like Little Fatty beat him to it. Alberto's cell was only a few doors down, but Alberto was a man with many enemies, and most likely was busy with his own problems. Jacob recalibrated his plan for Little Fatty and lowered the floating bars a few inches, folding his hands neatly behind his back.

Little Fatty came pounding around the corner, out of breath, and inhaled in preparation to deliver one final curse.

A metal bar streaked across the cell and drove through Fatty's fat head and out the other side. Fatty froze motionless on the landing, impaled through the forehead with his mouth open, his body hanging heavily from the bar. Jacob considered this scene for a moment before pushing the bar with its attached corpse over the banister onto the chaos below.

Jacob turned his wry smile back to check on Darrey, who continued to display the same deer-in-headlights look of shock.

The word "mayhem" didn't adequately describe what was happening on the floor of C-Block. Bodies and blood were flying all over the place, along with furniture, cell bars, chunks of concrete, and pretty much anything else that had any shape or weight behind it. Those with grudges went after each other with a vengeance while wielding a power none of them had grasped in their wildest dreams. As there was no lack of grudges in Westvale, a lot of accounts were being settled.

Jacob had no intention of being a part of that fray. These fools were missing the point; they were all free men now. What came before today should not be relevant to their new lives.

Jacob turned around and faced the back wall of his cell, and the cinderblocks burst away in a thunderous cacophony, clattering across the floor and through the tables of the chow hall on the other side. Jacob turned to Darrey, still seated in his bunk, mouth agape collecting flies.

"Look," Jacob said tersely. "You can rabbit on your own or you can come with me, but if you come, you have to be with me all the way. I say, you do. If that doesn't work for you, you are free to fuck off right now. Got it?"

Darrey swallowed and nodded. Jacob turned away without bothering to catch Darrey's expression, but even this didn't seem to be necessary, since he could somehow feel Darrey's relief. Darrey was probably every bit as powerful and dangerous as Jacob was now, but he was used to following orders, and probably didn't really want to be responsible for making decisions for himself. In fact, beyond his relief and obedience, Darrey indeed felt "with" Jacob in some strange new way. Jacob marked this sensation for later analysis.

The chow hall was deserted and dimly lit. Jacob thought about Darrey as he walked hurriedly through the center of the hall, long tables springing out of his way. He made a mental note to act more skilled, more experienced, and more powerful than other people. Fear itself was a much more versatile and useful tool than a gun, no matter how big your gun may be. Even if everyone had suddenly become Teks of equal power, it was likely that nobody was certain how their strength measured up. A simple bluff of Jacob being a stronger Tek seemed in order, which would be easy because he saw no reason to doubt it. Jacob always won at poker.

"Jacob!" called a prisoner named Julian, who had just burst open the door at the other end of the chow hall behind Jacob and Darrey. Julian was a large, black, bald man and had blood all over his face from some previous altercation. Jacob and Julian had agreed they hated each other, but Julian was a resident of B-Block, so nothing had needed to be sorted out between them.

Jacob paused, smiled, slowly turned about with a malicious grin on his face and locked eyes with Julian.

"Well, hello, Julian," hissed Jacob. Julian took a half step and blinked. "I forget, did we have a score to settle?" Jacob chided, as Darrey backed away. Jacob knew he couldn't count on Darrey's support in this kind of fight.

Both men eyed loose objects around the other and took a moment to experiment. Jacob noticed he really felt Julian's feelings when he glanced at the things Julian was looking at, and quickly inferred that Julian must be feeling his objects of attention as well. Somehow, Jacob could sense Julian's mood of hesitation and curiosity, in the same way he had sensed Darrey's feeling of relief. Julian should be getting a good whiff of Jacob's dominance.

Jacob cut the silence.

"So, what will it be, Julian? Are we not friends? Are you to be ripped in half today?" Jacob boasted with a smile as he twisted the metal and wood of one of the benches behind him. "Answer me now!" yelled Jacob insistently.

Jacob secretly relished Julian's wave of fear, even as he kept tight control on his own angry facade. Julian got a hold of himself and stuttered back to Jacob, "Naw, naw, we friends, Jacob, we cool. I wuz just wondering if you wanna roll together. The more the merrier'n all, ya know?" Julian gestured with his thumb to the main prison hall, where sounds of carnage still echoed.

Jacob had no idea what Julian was talking about, but there was no way he was communicating this to Julian, either through classical or magical means. Why anyone in this place, at this time, would choose to "roll together" was beyond him, but he knew Julian wouldn't offer friendship unless he had a damn good reason.

Without missing a beat, Jacob changed his stance and replied with an irritated smile, "Naturally, the mo' the merrier." He then strode up close to Julian in yet another display of fearlessness. "But I'll say this once. You can come with us, but this is my party. Never yours. Got it?"

Jacob didn't wait for Julian's nod of submission. He turned sharply and strode purposefully back down the same direction he was going before Julian had called his name. Jacob's face showed nothing but irritation, but as Darrey and Julian followed, Jacob could feel their relief, and again there was something more to it. Julian made Jacob feel like he knew everything.

Truthfully, Jacob didn't know exactly where he was going, as he had never been to this part of the prison, but the terrible noises were behind them, and that meant this was the correct direction. When the trio reached a dead end, Jacob simply ripped a hole through the wall and kept walking. Soon they tore into the outer yard, and saw the high, concrete, razor wire-crowned outer fence that marked the end of Westvale and the beginning of freedom. All three ran to the barrier and ripped it apart with rising excitement.

Jacob took careful note of how their powers interacted; parts of the wall where he felt other prisoners shoving in unison with him took barely a thought to come down. Obviously, there was strength in numbers, but suddenly Jacob's head was working overtime on a multitude of new questions. There was a quantity vs. quality question, a scalability question, and most importantly, a question of the impact of emotion.

Jacob filed these unknowns for later study, but whatever the answers, he was confident he was going to enjoy figuring them out. Darrey and Julian jumped ahead of him through the rubble and across the open fields into the dark, quiet woods. They both let loose whoops and screams of elation to be finally free of their concrete worlds. Happy to have not needed the debate about who would test the presence of guard tower fire, Jacob followed.

Jacob paused at the edge of the forest to improve on his comrade's noises and assert once again who should be feared. Jacob closed his eyes tightly, held out his fists in the air, and arched his head back as he prepared to be dramatic. With all his might, Jacob let out a long, loud, conquering scream of anger, fury, and power. The blood-curdling sound echoed through the forest and seemed to shake the ground Jacob was standing on.

Jacob was stunned by how potent and genuinely terrifying his little display had sounded. But he quickly returned his mask of anger before Julian and Darrey turned towards him with pale faces. Their fresh looks of terror made it clear his show had worked well. Too well. Better than his intent. Jacob quietly wondered why.

HOUR 6

Judy Bonner awoke peacefully next to Tom and slowly rose to a seated position. Always an early riser, Judy enjoyed waking Tom up using the aroma of breakfast.

Walking the short trip to the kitchen in their quaint little house, Judy strolled into the kitchen and got ready to watch herself make breakfast. It lately required so little preparation on her part, she barely had to put a thought into it. Things just made themselves using her arms.

Judy stopped short as she set foot on the linoleum of the kitchen. Her hands were obviously going for the pans in the bottom drawer to begin sautéing something, but today the drawer opened before her hands even made it there.

"Well, will you look at that," said Judy to herself.

Judy stayed at the edge of the kitchen, decided breakfast should continue to be made, and the shallow pan dislodged itself from the drawer and floated handle-first up to Judy's hand.

Judy paused and stared at the pan, turning it over in her hand for a minute, inspecting it for irregularities and confirming she wasn't dreaming. She knew the next step in breakfast would be to put the pan on the stove and turn it on, but now Judy wondered if she needed to even be in the kitchen at all.

Judy let go of the pan and it floated on over to the stove. She turned her attention to the gas knob and flame sprouted under the pan with a click.

"Well, this sure makes things easier," smiled Judy.

Judy continued to smirk as the dishes prepared breakfast. They weren't moving on their own, exactly; they just moved in the proper way to prepare eggs benedict. Some part of her knew how to make the dish, and the only thing she needed to think about was that breakfast would be fantastic.

Out of the side of her eye, Judy noticed Tom standing behind her in his robe with his mouth open.

"Well, don't be collectin' flies, Mr. Bonner," said Judy.

"That's…that's…impossible," Tom stammered.

"Obviously, it ain't," quipped Judy as another sliced English muffin made its way to the toaster.

Suddenly, the saucepan with the Hollandaise sauce didn't go where it needed to go. Judy's head filled with thoughts of Tom. His nervousness, his curiosity, his fear, and most of all his disagreement with Judy came out of nowhere into Judy's mind.

"Say what?" Judy asked reflexively, turning to Tom.

There was a great clatter as dishes, pans, and butter knives crashed to the ground in the kitchen, making a proper mess.

"Aw Tom, look what you did," said Judy, turning back sadly to the kitchen. I guess I'm not the only one in this house with powers anymore."

"I guess not," gulped Tom. "Judy, something must have happened. We should turn on the TV."

HOUR 7

Cory Nelson awoke with a smile in his cozy upstairs bedroom. Cory thought he heard something crashing outside, but more importantly, it was Saturday, which meant unlimited screen time, at least until Mom announced breakfast was ready. Double points for Mom and Dad not hogging the big TV in the morning.

Cory threw off the covers and bounded towards his open door. As he raced around the corner and into the hallway, the door moved before he passed it, as if on its own. Cory halted his charge and slowly turned to face the open door. The door swayed gently back and forth, but only where he thought it might sway. Cory wondered what would happen if the door moved sideways and was startled by the harsh creak of the door on its hinges.

"Mom?" Cory ventured, unsure of how urgent his voice should be.

Claire Nelson drifted into consciousness and reflexively turned to look at the iHome clock on her nightstand. Disgusted by the early hour it showed her, she turned away, and her clock went flying off her nightstand, carrying her phone with it to a clatter on the floor.

Claire turned back over, bleary eyed and mumbling, "what the hell," as Adam let out a particularly loud snore next to her. Assuming Cory probably yanked the cord, Claire first looked for Cory then spotted her phone, which slowly moved off the carpet, rose into the air and turned to face her. Claire stared transfixed at her gaping reflection in the hovering iPhone for a moment, clearly still dreaming yet somehow not waking up.

"Mom?" came Cory's voice again from the hallway, tinged with rising urgency.

Motherly instinct took control of Claire. Something was wrong and Cory was terrified. The phone fell to the floor as Claire threw off the covers and leapt out of bed simultaneously calling out, "Cory?"

Claire quickly discovered Cory in the hallway backing away from his room. Cory turned and saw his mother before sprinting towards her open arms. The two embraced and then went crashing to the floor in Claire's room, knocked off their feet by some unseen force.

The two lied still on the floor as Adam resumed his steady snore.

"Cory, do you want to tell Mommy what the heck is going on?" Claire said, trying to mask the fear in her voice.

"I can move the door, Mommy," Cory admitted.

"Okay," Claire thought about her phone on the floor. "I think I can move stuff too." Claire turned her head towards the pillow on the floor next to them and it slid towards her at the faintest suggestion that it should move. "I think we might be Teks now, Cory."

"Really?" said Cory, suddenly full of excitement. Cory turned his head towards the pillow, reached out his hand, and the pillow flew into it.

"Careful," said Claire, still nervous about the whole situation. She decided to push the pillow back away, but immediately there was a buzz, as if she had brushed an electric wire. Cory let go of the pillow with his hand and recoiled.

"Whoa," Claire and Cory said in unison.

After a pause, Claire said, "Let's try that again. Let's see who is stronger," appealing to Cory's competitive side.

"Sure!" Cory eagerly exclaimed. They disentangled and sat up, both looking at the pillow.

"You hold the pillow still and I'll try to move it. Got it?" asked Claire.

"Yes," smiled Cory, intently focused on the pillow.

Claire looked at the pillow and willed it to move towards her. Instantly she felt the buzzing, but rather than immediately release, she leaned into it, commanding the pillow to move. Her thoughts were invaded by Cory's thoughts, full of uncertainty and wonder, but also of the overriding thought that the pillow should stay where it is.

Claire wasn't about to be beaten by a 10-year-old. In her mind, she demanded the pillow move forward. She felt Cory immediately give way to her and the pillow moved.

"No fair!" protested Cory. "You said you didn't want it to move!"

"I said you should try to make it not move," but there was truth hidden in Cory's confusion. Contesting the pillow as a Tek was akin to telling Cory that it should move.

Claire felt Cory's will on the pillow again, so she immediately tried to move it. Now there was a confused thought at the forefront of Cory's mind, whether Mommy really wanted the pillow to move or not.

Claire found herself confused as well. The pillow didn't move.

Their experimentation was interrupted by the sound of Adam's snoring hitting a particularly loud note. Cory and Claire agreed that it was time to wake up Daddy, and that this task should be approached with extreme caution.

Hour 8

Keith rubbed his eyes, attempting to see around the glowing room. He had no idea where he was, but it reminded him of the Wizard's room from the Wizard of Oz, except that everything was glowing green so brightly that it hurt his eyes and it was hard to focus.

Keith cautiously approached the steps that led to where the great and powerful floating head of Oz surely lurked. There was plenty of green smoke, and the occasional burst of flame, but Keith couldn't locate any giant floating heads. There was, however, a strange high-pitched buzzing. Even without the head, Keith knew he was not alone. The great Oz was listening.

Keith felt that he was finally going to get some answers. After much searching, he had finally found an oracle that knew absolutely everything. Keith was sure of it, he had never been more sure of anything in his life. This thing would tell him what was going on. There was no doubting this oracle. It was here, and it was going to answer everything.

Keith cautiously stepped to the edge of the oracle, shaking with anticipation as green smoke swirled about.

Suddenly the buzzing noise stopped, and Keith knew it was time for him to ask his question.

Keith inhaled deeply, and then called out the question on the minds of just about the entire human population.

"What is going on?" Keith yelled.

The moment he finished pronouncing his final word, the oracle's answer arrived with a reverse echo from the depths of the brilliant green glow.

"Yes. What, *is* going on," stated the oracle with finality. The oracle's voice was male, deep, and definitive.

Disturbingly cryptic, Keith thought. Definitely truth, but also entirely useless. Keith hoped that all the oracle's answers were not like this. He decided to be more specific.

"Why can I move things with my mind?" queried Keith. He had always wondered how, exactly, his power worked, and he was sure that there was a rational, scientific explanation for it.

The oracle immediately replied, "Why? *I* can move things with *my* mind."

Keith paused. He hadn't asked the oracle about its powers, he and didn't understand how this answer had any relevance to his question. Keith decided to try again.

"What should I be doing? Where should I go?" Keith hoped the multiple questions would force the oracle to be more verbose.

"Yes, do that and go there," was the answer, completely serious, without a hint of sarcasm.

Keith was getting irritated. He began to think this oracle was a sham, and that the man behind the curtain didn't really know anything at all. He glanced at the green curtain, but decided he was going to try one more time before unmasking this fraudulent wizard.

Defeated, Keith asked, "Fine. So what should I do now?"

"Right now!" came the thundering response, almost before Keith had finished speaking. The room shook with the words and Keith tried to catch his balance.

Keith twitched and found himself back in his bed in his Seattle apartment, staring at the ceiling with his heart racing. Disoriented by the frustrating Wizard of Oz dream, he tried to figure out what had woken him.

There was the sound of a distant crash outside and then his entire apartment complex shuddered, as if some huge truck had just passed by.

Alarmed, Keith threw off the blanket and jumped out of bed, immediately registering a wave of fear washing over him. Something new was going on. And it was everywhere.

For lack of a better description, fear was in the air. Not the mild, eerie apprehension of dread, this fear was much more palpable, like the choking smoke of burning tires. It was everywhere, maybe coming from everyone. It was as if the world had decided everyone should be afraid now. Keith threw on a shirt and flipped on the TV at the foot of his bed.

The apocalypse. The images were on every channel. Some had emergency broadcast patterns, some simply rolled footage of buildings and bridges collapsing. Keith switched on Headline News, where a frazzled reporter in a crumpled shirt and tie was reading from various papers on his desk.

"… hours since the event. I repeat, every human on Earth, with few exceptions, over the age of around four or five, is now a Tek. We are advising all citizens to stay away from cities, buildings, prisons, or any other large concentrations of people. Above all, stay home. The death toll so far is…incomprehensible." The reporter's paper had begun floating in front of him as he read it. Embarrassed, he snatched the paper and put it back down on his pile.

Keith flipped through a few more channels. There was nobody on TV whose face did not wear shock or terror.

Keith immediately tried to test his power. He reached out to move the TV and was shocked to find that this suddenly required zero effort. He lifted the TV off its stand with barely a whim, flew it across the room and placed it down on the floor, remembering to unplug it at the last instant. No overwhelming sensory feedback, and no tug of the object's weight. Keith could still examine the insides of the TV like he could before, but it was now no longer required, as if the new power were separate from his old power.

Keith could only guess at the ramifications of this new development. Keith picked the TV back up with his mind and returned it to its place on the stand, plugging it back in with less than half a thought. Once again, the effortlessness of his power was astonishing.

He turned it on again with his remote.

"…avoid strong emotions and it is best to avert one's eyes from other people. If you are just joining us, you probably are already aware, it seems every adult on Earth gained the power of telekinesis at 1:31 a.m. Eastern Time. Anyone above the age of three can now kill at a distance with nothing more than an errant thought. Countries with the greatest inequalities have seen the greatest strife, as have cities, prisons…"

On some level, Keith felt relief. While he had known there were others like him, now that everyone on the planet had the same power, he was back to being just another one of the humans. He was no longer a monster, a freak, and he was not any sort of "chosen one."

Another few scenes of carnage on the TV made Keith change his mind. This was not relief.

Keith saw a video of a man dressed in black, walking away from the camera with his hands outstretched towards a freeway full of parked and/or wrecked cars. The cars flew out of the man's way as he flicked his fingers. Through the haze of the shaky camera phone video, Keith saw screaming faces in the windows.

The TV shuddered as Keith's anger momentarily escaped his control. He heard another crash outside. Keith knew that he was needed. Probably badly. People like that man in black had to be stopped. Keith prided himself on being non-violent, but he knew that he probably had a month of Tek experience more than the general population, so if anyone was going to challenge bad people doing bad things, he was probably one of the most qualified.

Keith finished dressing and prepared to take on the world. As horrible as the chaos was that had consumed the planet, he felt good for the first time in a long while. He had a purpose. He was going to go stop bad people from doing bad things, or more likely, he was going to die trying. He no longer had to hide his gift, and all that practicing might finally be worth something.

As he opened his door with his head held high, Keith felt like a superhero. He paused.

Keith closed his eyes and gingerly grabbed his skeletal structure with his mind. Keith had previously learned the hard way that mentally seizing one's entire body stops the lungs and heart, which is not desirable. Keith carefully lifted himself off the ground. Previously, Keith's own weight had made him strain with effort after only a few minutes of flying, but now that effort was no longer an issue, flight was probably going to be some serious fun. Keith decided to take things one step at a time, dropped back to the ground, and strode outside to take on the world.

HOUR 10

Toby's warning whistle, coming from high above in the trees, snapped Jacob from his furious musings. Someone was coming.

Jacob stretched and looked around the clearing. There were close to ten of them now, having gathered more followers throughout the night, all former Westvale inmates, mostly unfamiliar to Jacob.

Jacob motioned across his neck for everyone to be quiet. Even the new people had picked up on the rule to always be quiet around Jacob.

Frisco, the lanky informant with long blond hair, had snuck out of Westvale unscathed, and allegedly sought out Jacob earlier in the night. This would have been expected in the prior power dynamic, but surprising now that it was clear they were all equally powerful.

Frisco had positioned himself just behind and to the right of Jacob, which was a little presumptuous, as if he had declared himself Jacob's number 2.

The loud gossiping of two men came rumbling towards them as Jacob's group quietly fanned out behind him in a V formation.

"...you gotta know what you're doing. I mean like, really know. Your problem is you don't know how to know. Get it? Heh heh. What I'm saying is I know I know, and you don't know. Heh. Just joking. You know what I mean?"

"Uhuh," came the nonplussed response.

The speaker was obviously an idiot. And obviously irritating. Jacob weighed the cons of attacking first to avoid sullying his ranks with this ass.

"Hey which way will you go when you get to the road? I was thinking south, but then, that's because," the rambling thought was cut short as the pair entered the clearing, suddenly realizing they were face to face with ten men watching them.

The quiet one spoke first.

"Uh, huh huh… hi?" he ventured. "A Block," he identified himself. Jacob cut in.

"Nobody gives a shit about where your cage was in Westvale," he stated, pausing for simple minds to catch up. "There is only one thing we care about," Jacob paused again, this time for effect. "Are you with us or against us? You can join us or you can die. It's really simple. Honestly, I prefer the latter, but it is your choice." Jacob wasn't lying.

Barely hidden smiles crept across a few faces of the nine members of Jacob's group as they imagined ways these two would be ripped apart. Jacob didn't need to see the smiles to know his gang also preferred this option. Somehow the air was certain that if these two didn't immediately submit, their innards would quickly be adorning the tree trunks.

This time the loud one spoke first.

"Oh, hell yeah! We are with you one hundred percent!" said the irritating one, turning towards his companion for confirmation.

The quiet one had gone a bit ashen, but nodded in ascent. "Yeah, uh huh, definitely." At least he was aware of his surroundings.

"Great," said Jacob disappointedly. "I am Jacob. And this is *my* party, if you know what I mean." They did.

Truthfully, Jacob only had to flex his power once since leaving Westvale due to some unfinished business. Each new member assumed many bloodbaths before them, and dared not challenge a larger group.

"Let's move," commanded Jacob, mostly to break the tension and allow his new recruits to mingle. He snapped his fingers and Toby descended down from the tree. Jacob watched him carefully. Probably one of the first things people tried was to fly, and the shock of seizing yourself with your mind was probably one of the first lessons in how dangerous their new power was.

Toby, who had spent entirely too much time bragging about his climbing abilities while he was locked up, suddenly was showing something different to Jacob. This wasn't just being a Tek. Toby essentially ran down the tree like a monkey, far too fast to be grabbing himself with his mind, and far too effortlessly to be actually that good at climbing. Hell, Toby had to be pushing fifty. Nobody climbed like that.

Toby noticed Jacob was watching him as he descended.

"I know, right? Even I didn't think I was that good," beamed the old man.

"Indeed," snarled Jacob as he turned away. He didn't recall asking Toby a fucking thing.

HOUR 14

Night had fallen on Greenfield as Tom and Judy Bonner sat in their cozy living room, Tom on the couch and Judy in her chair, giggling like schoolchildren. A half-finished crochet doily hung in the air in the middle of the room, the needles still in it tugging at each other.

"You're gonna ruin it, Tom," said Judy, half-heartedly.

"Only if you don't let go," quipped Tom. The doily was not going to be accidentally ripped. Tom was sure of this because he could tell they both agreed that it was not going to happen.

"I'm not letting go," said Tom.

"Yes, you are," giggled Judy.

Tom was in some sort of argument with Judy, where he had the constant choice of whether to accede to her demands or stand firm in his desires. And this argument was accompanied by a buzzing, like an electric hum in his mind, varying in intensity with his thoughts and her thoughts.

"Well, I guess we'll just sit here all night," chuckled Judy.

Tom's thoughts strayed to the horrors they saw earlier on TV, before deciding to turn it off. Tom had never been more thankful to live in a secluded part of the world. This new power was having terrible consequences for folks.

"Hah!" said Judy, as the yarn and needles flew over to her hand.

Before Tom had a chance to react, a sound came from outside that caused both Bonners to freeze. Tom's hair stood on end as a long, mournful howl, joined by several other howls, filled the house. The howling was back, this time much closer, and it sounded like a lot more dogs.

"Edgar's monsters," whispered Judy.

Judy got up and went to the window as Tom's mind raced. He got up and hurried into the bedroom to grab his shotgun and pulled a few shells from the box in the closet. All he had was buckshot, since he only ever used it for bird hunting, but it was the only weapon he owned, and it was better than nothing.

Tom paused and looked at the gun. Or was it?

Tom imagined tearing a wolf in two with his mind and was pretty sure that would be more effective than bird pellets.

As he came out of the bedroom, Judy called out to him, "Look!" and pointed out the window.

Tom joined Judy at their living room window and looked out across their field to see a car coming down the road towards them in the distance with some sort of weird sparkling red fog tailing it. Tom went outside to get a better look.

Only headlights were visible at this point, but Tom knew it was Edgar barreling towards them. The truck was still quite a ways away, but Tom could tell from where he was standing that Edgar had the old white pickup's pedal to the metal. Swirling and floating along behind it was a roiling fog, highlighted by the vehicle's red tail lights. Tom squinted into the distance.

Tom felt his heart sink as he slowly began to understand what he was looking at. The fog was composed of dozens of pairs of tiny red lights, following the truck like a swarm of fireflies.

"Stay inside, Judy!" Tom called back to his wife, his voice stumbling. He looked down at his bird-hunting shotgun. That was no fog, and those sure as hell weren't fireflies. Those were eyes. Shining red eyes.

Tom quickly tried to estimate the number of monsters approaching. There were somewhere in the neighborhood of fifty sets of demonic eyes. Shotgun or Tek powers, the choice of weapon didn't seem as important anymore. That was a lot of eyes.

Edgar's truck screeched off the road and threw up dirt as the driver gunned the engine towards the Bonner residence. The cloud of red eyes had just reached the Bonner's lower fields, still a few football field lengths away, but they were closing fast. Tom started worrying that Edgar was going to ram their house, but Edgar slammed on the brakes and leaped out of his car as he arrived in an explosion of dust and gravel.

Edgar did not look well. He was shaking, covered in sweat, his left arm was limp and bloody. Tom couldn't tell where the blood was coming from, but most of it looked dry. Edgar's good hand gripped a .22 caliber rifle with white knuckles.

"Tom! Thank God! Git your guns! They're a-comin'! The goddamn wolves are coming! I'm down to mah last pea-shooter! Git yer guns!"

Tom froze on his porch, staring wide-eyed at Edgar.

"Shit Edgar! We only got the one and it's for huntin' ducks!" Tom showed the shotgun to Edgar as his eyes drifted back towards the wolves, whose lumbering shapes were now clearly attached to the glowing dots. "Shouldn't we, uh, get the hell out of here? We can all squeeze in my truck and-"

"And what Tom?" Edgar turned crossly towards him, as he grabbed a box of bullets from the bed of his truck and sat down in front of his front bumper. "Drive back thru em? Naw, you gotta kill em! I killed a slew of 'em at my place before I had to get outta there. They hate it when you shoot 'em," Edgar grinned as he frantically reloaded his small rifle.

"Forget about holing up, they just come through the windows. Use yer brain powers if they get too close! Use it like a shield!" Edgar shouted as he reloaded.

Seeing how Edgar was obviously the resident expert on demon wolves, Tom quickly agreed to follow his advice and prepared to make a stand. Tom ran inside and grabbed the box of shells for his shotgun. Using Tek powers as a shield was obviously a great idea. The power could change targets as fast as one could shift focus. A person could hold probably hold off an entire horde of wolves with Tek magic, and this wasn't quite a horde.

"Tom?" Judy asked as he walked by fumbling with his box of bullets. "Tom!" There was a loud crack from outside, where Edgar was already taking shots at the approaching wolves.

"Stay inside, Judy, and if any wolves get inside, uh, use your brain." This was the best advice Tom could give Judy, since she was obviously more talented in that department, and regardless, he had no more weapons for her. Judy blinked with an open mouth and Tom didn't wait for a response before heading outside and joining Edgar in the bed of his truck.

As the wolves got closer, Tom began to question their whole strategy. The color began to drain from Tom's face as the monsters came into full view.

These wolves were big—very big. They stood roughly five feet tall, and were a uniform, creepy grey. Not a one had a single patch of fur that was any color but the same flat grey, in sharp contrast to their mystically glowing blood-red eyes. The wolves were all panting as they loped towards Tom's home, showing glistening rows of teeth.

Edgar's rifle cracked again and shocked Tom back into reality. The yelp and stumble of Edgar's target reminded Tom that these were mortal wolves, and that he should be firing as fast as he could manage.

Tom figured his double-barreled shotgun should at least slow down or deter a few wolves as the wolves closed in, now about fifty feet away. The gun's clumsy and slow reload, two shells at a time, was weighing heavily on Tom's mind as he took aim.

"Tom!" Judy called from inside the house.

Tom fired with a mighty boom. The blast was a big, new noise to the wolves, and though the pack was still more than 50 yards away, it made them all do a little skip. The wolf at the end of his sights turned away with a yelp, pawing at its face. The huge pack howled furiously and renewed its charge. Their prey was now within sight.

"Edgar! Thomas Bonner!" Judy yammered from behind the glass. Tom could hear rapping on the window, could feel Judy trying to get his attention with her brain powers, and the expression of irritation on Edgar's face matched what Tom was thinking: *Not now, woman!*

Tom fired again quickly, trying to ensure he had enough time to reload before the wolves were upon him. Tom snapped his gun open and pulled out the spent shells as fast as he could manage with his shaky hands. Edgar's rifle cracked again and again. As he was shoving in the new shells, Tom glanced up and saw the wolves were less than twenty yards away and closing fast. Tom's mind raced. If he had to look down to reload, would he be able to see wolves jumping on top of him? Should he and Edgar assume attack and defense roles instead? He had only seconds to think.

"Guys!" yelled Judy, as the entire truck rocked to the side, sending the two men toppling over each other inside the truck bed. Judy obviously had shoved them with her brain, and Tom scrambled up, whipping his head towards Judy, wondering what the hell could be more important than killing wolves at this instant.

Judy was standing outside on the porch with both hands outstretched pointing at the wolves but facing the truck. "Look! They're retreating!" she called.

Tom sat up and turned back toward the wolves, catching sight of the last few sets of red eyes turning away from him. The rest of the wolves had already turned and were proceeding directly away from the truck at the same loping gait with which they had advanced moments before. Tom was dumbfounded. It was a miracle.

"Well, I'll be God-damned," Edgar said breathlessly.

Tom looked back towards Judy in the window and saw her self-satisfied smile. This was no miracle. This was Judy.

"Hey Edgar," said Tom. Edgar turned towards him. "Something tells me we need to go have a little talk with Judy about what just happened."

As Tom and Edgar shakily pulled themselves together and crawled out of the truck, Tom realized he had been breathing through his mouth this whole time. The fight with the wolves had not improved Edgar's stench.

Hour 20

When Keith ventured from his apartment that morning, he had expected a face full of a world in chaos, but the reality was more that the world was in hiding.

Keith's apartment was on a hillside near downtown Seattle, but far enough away to be out of range of any large buildings. Since the news said heavily populated areas were hardest hit by the destruction, Keith had decided to walk straight towards downtown. He still worried that flying would draw too much attention to him.

A nagging question lingered in the back of Keith's mind as he strolled through the deserted streets. How exactly was he supposed to find bad people who needed to be stopped? Was this even feasible? Keith wondered what his chances were of randomly encountering a bad guy in the middle of doing bad things.

Finally, while wandering aimlessly in the streets of Seattle in the afternoon, he heard the sound of screams. With a small kick of adrenaline, Keith ran towards the uproar.

Rounding a corner, Keith saw exactly the scene of violence for which he had been searching.

A pudgy, bald man with a black X painted on his face was chasing after a group of seven or eight people. The bald man was cackling quite madly as he waved his arm and launched a car at the crowd. A tired-looking man in a dusty brown business suit whirled, put up his hand and the car was deflected to the left.

"What the hell is wrong with you!?" demanded the man.

"Just leave us alone!" bawled a woman in the group. She was obviously the most shaken, but the expressions of the group varied widely between terror and irritation.

The bald man laughed in a higher key and swung both of his arms towards the group, sending two more cars towards them. They were again deflected amid a few screams as the group slowly fled.

"Now or never," thought Keith. He flanked the party and shouted "Stop!" in the most heroic way possible. His voice echoed.

The bald man turned towards him with an angry sneer on his face. The fleeing group also stopped fleeing and turned towards him. Neither party was sure of what to expect from Keith. Neither was Keith.

The bald man decided it was time to put Keith's money where his mouth was. He glanced sideways, reached out his arm and tossed a car in Keith's direction.

Keith knew he could just deflect the car like the people were doing, but that was this guy's game, and Keith didn't want to play.

Instead, he reached out his arm and grabbed the car with his mind and flipped it flying towards the bald man. He didn't let go of the car with his mind either, as he didn't want to get into a car-tossing match.

The bald man immediately grabbed the car with his mind as Keith bore it down upon him. Instantly, the same electricity that Keith felt with Rupert shocked both participants. Keith was ready for it—the man named Lester, not so much.

The weird electric feeling of forced telepathy flooded Keith's mind. Since there was no longer any effort associated with using his power, Keith could focus on his opponent.

Lester's mind was ugly, full of shame, fear, and anger. The X on his face was actually dried blood, painted by Lester from one of his victims to make him seem scarier both to himself and to others. Lester was self-conscious about this X, unsure if people would see it as he intended, a scary mask, or if people would think it looked stupid. Also, foremost on Lester's mind was his own severe weariness, as well as a nagging concern about how he was going to locate more of some drug he desperately wanted.

Keith could tell his own mind was terrifying Lester. Keith was at peace, confident, excited, but not in any way scared by him. Keith knew he had an advantage in this fight, and he could tell Lester felt it too. Lester had made a huge mistake.

They only had seconds to evaluate each other's minds before the minds of the crowd interrupted them.

Keith was overwhelmed by the instant power coming from the seven people who had just ceased being terrorized by Lester. Seven different thoughts and opinions flooded Keith's mind. Most were full of relief and about how glorious and noble Keith was, a few promoted swift, hot revenge against their tormentor, but all seven were confident that Keith was going to be triumphant in this battle.

In a flash, Lester disengaged, jumped out of the way of the car, and high-tailed it away as fast as his chubby little legs could carry him.

Right away, Keith felt a push from the crowd to go after him, to hunt that son-of-a-bitch down, to quickly kill Lester before he could hurt anyone else. Keith held out his arms for balance as his body was pushed forward by the crowd, but he dug in his heels and made it clear this was not happening. The crowd, some of whom agreed with Keith's nonviolent point of view, conceded immediately.

Keith had made up his mind that murder was never going to be part of his plan. He had been preparing himself to take another human life if it came down to it, but hunting down and slaughtering someone for something they did was, in Keith's opinion, simply not right. He knew that he very possibly might be saving future lives by killing someone who might kill again, but this logic could never justify premeditated murder.

"Thank you, thank you … Keith, right?" said the man in the brown business suit as he stepped forward out of the group. Keith was surprised that the man knew his name, but considering that he had just conflicted with the entire crowd, they probably all knew his name. Sheepishly, Keith realized that this meant that he should also know the man's name, but he wasn't paying attention when the conflict had happened. Plus, Keith was never good with names anyway.

"Uh … you're welcome, uh …" Keith led as he offered his hand.

"Nathan," the man finished as he shook Keith's hand. "If you hadn't come along, I don't know how long we would have been running from that jackass." The rest of the crowd beamed smiles of relief at Keith. "I mean, we knew someone had to stand up to him, but he was just so damned freaky. His thoughts …" Nathan trailed off, looking in the direction Lester ran, still holding Keith's hand.

After talking to the group for a little while, Keith realized the group probably wasn't in as much danger as it had appeared. Purportedly, the three men in the group were just waiting for the right opportunity to confront Lester, but none of them wanted to be the one to do it.

"If Tammy hadn't been bawling the whole time, we probably would have taken care of it earlier," said Nathan.

"Oh, fuck you Nathan!" said Tammy, still wiping her tears.

"Yeah, fuck you Nathan," said Jim. "Nobody was stopping you from being the hero. You were just as scared as the rest of us."

"Hey, I didn't see you stepping up," said Nathan.

Several more arguments began to break out among the group. Keith decided to take his leave.

"Okay, so stay safe," said Keith over the top of the noise, unsure of what advice to give.

"Wait, uh, we're coming with you," Nathan said, suddenly worried again that Keith was about to leave them. This tone of alarm was quickly picked up by the rest of the group, who all joined with Nathan, projecting that Keith was not going to be leaving them.

Keith felt his feet rooted to the floor by the small group of people and wondered how the hell Rupert had managed to lose that giant crowd the week before.

"Look, uh, you guys don't need me," Keith lied. In truth, Keith just wanted to continue to explore the rules and boundaries of this new world, and he felt he just couldn't do that if he was busy looking after a bunch of people's safety.

His lie did not go over well. Everyone in the group could see right through the lie, even without powers, as Keith was notoriously bad at lying. Most were saddened, and some were angered that Keith was trying to abandon them.

Nathan stepped forward again, flushed. "Look, Keith, now we all know that is not true. C'mon, man, you can tell we all need a leader here."

Keith saw his opportunity.

"Then, by the power vested in me, I now declare you, Nathan, the undisputed leader of this group!" Keith turned and began striding away before the confused bunch had time to process what he had said. Keith was obviously the authority on these matters; who were they to challenge his words?

Keith stole a quick glance over his shoulder to check on the group as he walked away. Everyone was focused on Nathan, who was trying to hide a smile. Everyone still looked a little perplexed, but overall, it looked like they bought it. Nathan now had the support of the group.

It wasn't like what Keith had said was a lie. In fact, there seemed to be something significant about having a leader. Keith wasn't sure how Tek leadership worked, but he did feel as if he was riding a bucking bronco when this group had his back. Their numbers had power that they didn't realize; they just needed focus.

As Keith walked back towards his apartment, he hoped his building was still standing. He could totally go for a bath right now.

HOUR 30

The morning of the second day was calmer in the Nelson's household. Adam and Cory were asleep on the couch in the living room. Claire was awake in the recliner, staring numbly in silence as the TV continued to quietly describe the mayhem of the previous night. Some places had lost power, but the lights had thankfully never gone out in New York.

Looking over at her sleeping family, Claire wondered what kind of future they all now faced. In the past, everything had made sense, but now there were no rules, no laws, and worst of all, no control. What good are police when their guns are no longer effective? Claire stood and walked into the kitchen as the light from the first sun shone in through the crack in the drapes.

Claire fetched a glass and poured herself a glass of water. As she sipped, gazing thoughtfully through the kitchen window, she spotted movement in the street in the front of her house. Adjusting the kitchen curtain, Claire leaned closer and caught sight of a young man standing at the edge of their driveway, facing the house. He was looking at her.

Claire's heart skipped as adrenaline made her skin tingle. The man looked grubby, dirty, all kinds of scary. Skinny, white, and unshaven, he had dreadlocks, two nose rings, and worst of all, his eyes were fixed on Claire through the window. And he was smiling. Claire backed away from the window, nervously calling out to her family, "honey …" The man began approaching the house.

Claire snapped into action and rushed into the living room, shaking her sleeping family while urgently whispering, "Adam, Cory, wake up! Someone is outside."

Adam woke on the couch in a panic. Claire, who doesn't panic, sounded panicky, so it was clearly time to panic. He barely had time to get his bearings before a horrendous creaking sound came from the door.

"Upstairs!" commanded Adam, figuring they might be able to hide from the intruder, unaware that Claire had already been spotted.

Cory used all fours to race up the stairs with all the nimbleness of someone who routinely took the stairs at top speed. Claire hustled after him as fast as she could manage, unhindered by her sweats.

Adam hesitated, not knowing whether to stand and fight or if he should stick with his family.

The Nelson's door exploded inward, sending shards of wood across the entryway. Adam instinctively held out his hand and willed the splinters away from him. Surprisingly, the splinters obeyed, reflecting off an invisible sphere around him.

A raspy, high-pitched voice came drifting through the rubble, "oh missus hot lips," it cooed.

Upstairs, Claire shoved Cory into the bathroom attached to the master bedroom. Cory turned his fearful face towards her as Claire hissed, "Hide!" and shut the door.

Adam blinked at the intruder through the falling splinters. The man couldn't have been more than twenty or twenty-five years of age. He had pale white skin, face jewelry, and a large tattoo on his neck. He wore a round black hat, out of which fell matted dreadlocks of various lengths, all of which merged with the man's greasy facial hair in the most disorganized way possible.

Adam immediately lost his nerve. Before he had gone to sleep the night before, he was feeling confident of his ability to control a floating pillow. Now, suddenly, he was expected to match Tek powers against a malicious hooligan who blew doors apart on a whim?

Adam turned and ran up the stairs after his family. Turning back as he reached the top of the stairs, Adam locked eyes for a moment with the man gingerly stepping through his frayed hole of a doorway. Adam's stomach turned as he ran into the bedroom and locked the door behind him.

"Aww, you don't want to play?" chided the intruder as he skipped up the stairs, following the family.

Adam stood on the other side of the bedroom door with his mind locked on every inch of it. Claire stood in the far corner of the room with her eyes wide and the bedroom lamp in her hand. Adam wasn't sure what Claire was planning on doing with the lamp, but he knew, just as Claire knew, just as the bad man probably knew, that the Nelsons were not a threat.

The door lurched as the man reached it.

"Oh really?" came the raspy voice from the other side of the door. "You think you can stop me?"

The door flexed and creaked as the mind of the intruder pressed into Adam's thoughts. Adam knew people called the man Kessler, and Kessler was angry. Kessler had recently discovered that he could get his way, and he intended to get it.

The door squeaked louder as its hinges snapped and Adam helplessly fought against Kessler's mind. Kessler was unafraid, Kessler intended to do something horrible to Claire, and Kessler was confident in his ability to do it. Adam knew he wouldn't be able to stop it.

Adam staggered back and watched with horror as the door ripped off its hinges. It floated between the two men for a moment before Kessler tossed it to the side where it crashed to the floor.

Kessler took control.

"Stop!" Kessler commanded as he strode into the bedroom with his hand outstretched. He pointed at Adam's throat and made a claw with his hand.

Adam, who was waiting to hear Kessler's demands, suddenly clutched at his own neck as he was lifted off the floor.

"Now," dictated Kessler, "this is how it is gonna work. You and your stupid little powers are going to wait right there." Adam's hovering body, led by his neck first, flew back and slammed against the wall. Adam could feel Kessler's mind on his neck, and any time he tried to resist with his mind, Kessler would notice and give his neck a squeeze, so he was forced to hang help-less in mid-air, pinned on the wall.

"And you, my fine lady," said Kessler as he turned towards Claire, who had dropped the lamp in fear and was watching her husband on the wall with wide eyes. "You're going to lie right—here!" Kessler flicked his other hand out and Claire's body flew up from the ground and landed outstretched on the bed. "And you're going to do exactly what I want you to do."

Kessler licked his lips with a big smile on his face as Claire, unable to move, watched with horror as her sweatpants slowly slid down her legs. Adam tried to yell but immediately had his throat constricted.

Kessler heard a snap and followed the noise to where the bedroom connected to the bathroom. In the doorway stood Cory, who held a broken wooden action figure in his hands. His face, lined with tears, was bright red with rage, and his eyes were locked on Kessler.

"No!" roared Cory, and Kessler was launched from where he stood up and through the wall and roof. In that split second, Kessler's mind attempted a protest, but there was no defending against Cory's rage, which was pure and focused, undistracted by logic or doubt, unhindered by an adult's mental chatter.

Right before three layers of wood, wire, insulation, and roof-ing shredded his body on its way toward the sky, Kessler's last thought was that this child was correct, he was a bad man and should die now.

HOUR 33

"Now!" yelled Jacob from his hidden spot in the bushes.

The pig line was less than 100 meters away, arranged in the classic car-plus-shotgun formation, clearly intending to confront Jacob's group, yet inexplicably oblivious to the uselessness of their guns. Apparently set up protecting a gas station in the middle of fucking nowhere, the officers were anything but threatening. Some were covered with white dust, some were splattered with blood, but all had looks of shock on their faces. These assholes had lost before the battle began.

"Leave no pig left alive!" Jacob roared and charged from the bushes along with over twenty former clink mates who had pledged allegiance to him since his Westvale exodus. Just as before at Westvale's fence, Jacob's roar was amplified by his men. His men were expecting it, and it sounded like a megaphone. This should be fun.

A volley of shots rang out as Jacob's army closed the distance from the edge of the forest to the road. Bullets ricocheted across and between the charging throng. The thought that Jacob had ensured everyone clearly understood the night before briefly flashed across his mind: "bullets bounce off of us." The only other piece of strategy that Jacob had tried to sear into his followers' simple minds was that any troubles should be immediately referred to him. There was nothing Jacob couldn't handle, and he suspected this may be true simply because he expected it to be true.

Waves of fear came pouring out from the officers. The force of the emotion took all the prisoners by surprise, almost causing a stumble in the charge, but then immediately amplifying their own ferocity.

Jacob flicked his wrist and one of the first cop cars launched towards the heavens as a husky black cop behind it fell to the ground and two other cops backed away exposed, one of them futilely firing her obsolete tool of yesterday, and all three with matching expressions of terror.

Julian roared and brought his fists down in front of him as the chest of a grounded officer caved in ten feet in front of him. Lyle clawed at the air as the limbs twisted off another shrieking pig. Screams and shouts punctuated the chaos as Jacob's prison warriors navigated the bloody fray, many repeating their Tek strategy from Westvale's pit, carefully holding onto their own space as they pushed against others.

Jacob jumped up on a flipped car, scanning the whole battle. Seeing some of his men not participating, he danced through the fray leaping up behind Kenny, who appeared to just be watching with a sickened sheen on his face.

"Problem, Kenny?" asked Jacob. Kenny jumped.

"No, uh, no problem boss," he stammered.

"Then get your ass in there," said Jacob as he shoved Kenny with his hand. This was the gentler option and Kenny had better know it. Kenny did not want to be shoved by Jacob's mind.

Alarm snapped Jacob's head around. There was a problem. His men needed him. Jacob was unsure whether someone had called out for him or if he just sensed it, or if there was even a difference.

Jacob bounded across the combat zone as most of his men continued dominating the battlefield. Jumping effortlessly on top of a car, he assessed the situation that had called to him.

A large cop with a bald head and a thick, brown mustache had planted his feet and was swinging his fists in front of him. Jacob's men were bouncing off the air about five feet from him. A big thug named Clyde took an invisible fist to the torso. Clyde flew sideways, his face twisting not in pain but in rage.

"Who the fuck do you think you are?" asked Jacob, squatting on top of the patrol car, focusing his penetrating gaze on the man's eyes.

Jacob's men paused their assault and turned towards their leader.

"Police Chief Harold Byron," the man stated confidently. "And who the fuck are you?"

Jacob smiled. *Wrong question, Harold.*

The car Jacob was crouching on flew backwards as he extended his legs to touch the ground. Jacob strode towards Harold the Police Chief, feeling Harold's scramble to stop Jacob's advance. Harold believed he couldn't be killed, but there was more there. Harold's men thought Harold was unkillable too, or at least, the men that were still left did.

"I" said Jacob, with a dramatic pause, as he felt the anticipation swell in his own men. "Am," he continued, seizing on the fear rising in Harold's mind.

"Jacob!" snarled Jacob as he plunged the dagger of his hands at Harold's heart. Harold's defenses buckled as the force of certainty behind Jacob's words eclipsed Harold's dubious hold on his immortality. The sickening sound of metal slicing bone and flesh erupted from the center of Harold's body where Jacob's fingers pointed.

A half second later, Harold fell backwards, blood dribbling from his mouth, accompanied by a cheer from Jacob's men.

Later, Jacob lounged in one of the few patrol cars left undamaged, reflecting on what could be learned from the battle while his men played in the messy aftermath. All the cops were dead. Jacob's men only suffered minor injuries.

The clearest lesson was the importance of leadership. The battle with Harold might have gone differently if Harold had been the one with an army of loyal followers who thought he was invincible.

The sound of a shotgun going off distracted Jacob for a second. Subsequent chuckles allowed him to return to his musing as he absently dabbed his middle finger in the pool of blood on the passenger seat.

It was also clear that though Jacob could ride the wave of his men's thoughts, he had to be careful not to let them control him. Although displays of brutality were good for morale, he should maintain them as displays only. His men's enthusiasm must not affect his objectivity, much less his actual actions.

Jacob caught sight of a few of his men casting glances in his direction, obviously wondering what their next move was. Jacob turned back to his thoughts, with just enough disdain in his expression to signal that bothering him would not be wise.

The last thing that warranted further study was the sound of Harold's chest being punctured. It had the metallic twang of a sword. Jacob had been thinking of something he saw in a Terminator movie, where a sci-fi machine had turned its hands into swords. Jacob looked at his hand again and wondered if the metallic sheen it had was real or just in his head.

DAY 2

"Get a move on, Tom!" hollered Judy from the cab of the truck. It was Sunday, and they were heading to church, but not for the usual reasons. A few hours ago, Bailey had called and let them know that the townsfolk were gathering at the church to weather the storm.

"Wut ya think he's doin?" asked Edgar, sitting in his parked truck next to the Bonners' pickup.

"Oh, you know Tom. This or that." Judy honked the horn as Tom struggled out the door lugging a large brown suitcase.

"C'mon, Tom, Meadowview ain't but an hour away," said Judy.

"Dammit Judy, who knows what they have there or when we will be back," Tom retorted as he tossed his suitcase in the back of the truck. Rounding the truck, Tom opened the passenger side door and jumped in as Judy started the engine. Tom slammed the passenger door as the two trucks began making their way down Tom's gravel driveway.

"And what's the rush, anyway? It ain't like the church is going anywhere," said Tom.

"You saw the news too, Tom," said Judy. They had seen a story about a gang of thugs banding together and tearing through some rural community down south. It was clear that it wasn't good to be alone.

After about five minutes of driving, Tom broke the silence.

"Hon, do you mind going over the wolves with me again?" Tom asked. They had all discussed it the day before, but it was still difficult for Judy to put into words.

"Well, so you and Edgar were making the wolves charge. What more do you need to know?" asked Judy.

"Now now, you know Edgar and I didn't want to be attacked by wolves. So, what do you mean, 'making them charge?'" asked Tom. Judy looked up from the road as she thought about this for a moment.

"I guess I'm not really sure. Whatever you two guys with guns were doing, it was making the wolves very angry," snarked Judy. Tom frowned.

"And then you just made them go away?" asked Tom.

"To tell the truth, hon, I tried to make them go away when they were far away, but they didn't listen. They were all so focused on you guys," said Judy, pausing for a moment. "You guys were focused on each other, actually."

"So, rocking our boat broke their focus?" asked Tom, his brow furrowing. Judy pondered a moment again.

"I think so," said Judy. "As soon as I stopped you guys from doing whatever it was you were doing, they listened to me right away."

Tom's face retained its frown, but apparently was satisfied with this answer, as another five minutes of silence passed as Illinois farmlands scrolled by.

"One more thing," Tom said.

"Yes hon?" Judy replied.

"What the Sam hell is up with Edgar's smell? I mean, the guy just got out of the shower, right? How is it even possible to smell that bad that quickly? Does he not understand soap?"

Judy had to smile, although she didn't have any answers this time. Edgar had suffered a nasty bite on his arm before heading to the Bonners. Edgar had taken a shower and cleaned himself up, but he still stank like Edgar. Judy had caught Tom trying to covertly locate the scent on Edgar with his nose.

"Well…you know how I can magically cook now? Maybe Edgar just knows how to magically smell somehow," was her answer. She knew she was grasping at straws, but that foul odor simply could not be normal.

"Damn, Judy, you think Edgar wants to reek like rotting death?" asked Tom.

"Obviously, he can't smell it, Tom," chided Judy. "And I still don't know what want has to do with it. Remember you guys didn't want to be attacked by wolves, right?"

A few more minutes in silence passed.

"You don't suppose those wolves were rabid, do you?" asked Tom.

"Of course not," stated Judy. "Those dogs did not act crazy."

"What about werewolves?" asked Tom. This made Judy pause.

"Well, it couldn't hurt to keep on eye on Edgar at the next full moon," smiled Judy. They both knew she was only half-joking.

The rest of the drive to the Meadowview Church was quiet.

As both trucks arrived in the dusty parking lot, Tom and Judy saw Reverend Bailey outside the church greeting people with a smile, like it was any other Sunday at church. Tom found himself wishing for Reverend Foster, as Bailey's grin seemed awfully insensitive, considering all the death and destruction.

Still, at least it was a smile. To see one did make Tom feel good.

As the three approached the Reverend, the doors of a station wagon slammed shut as the Mitchell family eyed them suspiciously. Although the Mitchell family were not close to the Bonners, the usual courtesy between them was conspicuously absent.

The Reverend caught sight of this and snapped his fingers.

"Over here, Danny," Bailey said, getting the attention of the Mitchell boy. "You too there Bonners, look over here for a moment."

The Reverend continued. "Welcome to the Meadowview Sanctuary, where God is offering to look after you and your family. Please, before you enter, I ask everyone to please try to budge this cross with their minds." Bailey gestured to the wooden cross above the door.

Tom followed instructions and tried to give the cross a little tug.

The reason for this suddenly became clear. Bailey was holding onto the cross in place with his mind, and any effort to move it caused the aggressor to feel Bailey's mind.

What Tom felt from Bailey was an astounding degree of confidence. It was as if every member of his congregation, over a dozen at least, had added their strength to Bailey's cross as they passed under it. It was Bailey's cross, and Tom was not moving it. This fact was somehow chiseled in stone by many different hands.

Tom saw now why the reverend was smiling. There was security here, there was safety here, there was strength and power under the archway of the church. For the first time in weeks, it felt like everything was going to be okay. Uncertainty had been banished; it was clear that they all could rely on Bailey's strength.

"Well, I'll be," mumbled Tom, as he joined Judy and Edgar in giant, toothy grins. He had not expected Reverend Bailey to ever help anyone with anything, but here it was, a sanctuary, a strong sanctuary, and he had the young, goofy reverend to thank for it.

"Thank the Lord!" Judy blurted, with tears welling up in her eyes. Tom didn't know whether or not the Lord should be thanked, but he knew Mr. Bailey should be.

"Yessir. Thank the Lord," said Tom to Bailey, hoping his expression conveyed his gratitude. Bailey's grin was permanent.

"Please, make yourself at home," said Bailey. "There is plenty of coffee and plenty of empty cots in the back." The reverend caught sight of more cars arriving and waved the Bonners inside along with the smiling pack of Mitchells. The man was busy.

Tom and Judy opened the door and found the stale wooden air of the church mixed with the smell of relief and coffee. Immediately, they were met with smiling faces of families and set about their greetings. A few families did not smile, but mostly the mood was one of comfort.

As someone handed him a pile of blankets, Tom caught sight of Bailey pulling Edgar aside before he got to the door of the church. As Judy continued her skillful socializing, Tom glanced through the door as another family entered. It looked like Bailey was right in Edgar's face with his finger out, like he was scolding Edgar, and Edgar was looking at the ground and nodding.

Bailey turned back around and resumed his greeting duties.'

Later, after Tom and Judy had claimed a cot and were checking out the coffee situation, they spotted Edgar awkwardly milling about. Tom approached, dying of curiosity. "Hey Edgar, what did Bailey say to you?"

"He tells me I don't smell no more," Edgar looked up to Tom. "Tom, was I a'smellin?"

Tom looked to Judy for support, who looked away.

"Well, uh," Tom started.

"Dang it, Tom, why didn't ya say nuthin? You know mah nose don't work so good!" Edgar grumbled and moved away from the Bonners.

Tom wasn't sure why Edgar thought he would have any idea about his nasal handicap. The smell was just something he had accepted about Edgar years ago, as did most everyone else. Watching Edgar's angry retreat, Tom felt bad about never saying anything.

"Bailey was right," Judy stated.

"Huh? What?" Tom asked.

Judy nodded meaningfully in Edgar's direction.

Tom realized what she meant. Edgar no longer stank to high heaven. There was no trace of the famous Edgar odor, and Tom had been right next to him. Bailey had accomplished with a few words what a hot shower could not.

The Bonners reached the back of the church where the relief of the townsfolk was palpable. Aside from the occasional slip-up where someone—usually some kid—accidentally shoved something with their mind, it felt safe. Finally.

DAY 4

Cory Nelson stared at the ceiling of his dark bedroom. He had been trying to sleep for almost an hour now, but there were just too many exciting possibilities cavorting around in his head. Even though he spent most of the last few days practicing his new Tek powers, he still could not get enough. He wanted to dance, he wanted to toss everything around, he wanted to fly. Cory's room was a mess, and Mom had thrown a fit when she caught him juggling with the recliner.

Cory frustratingly turned on his side and tried to put the future out of his mind. He wondered what his parents were doing. They were staying in the guest room next to Cory's bedroom, since the hole in the ceiling known as "Cory's Wrath," as they liked to call it, had made their bedroom too cold to sleep in.

Cory tried to push those thoughts from his mind as well. Although saving the day and rescuing his parents made him feel good, feeling the bad man's thoughts did not. There were way too many things going on there that he didn't understand and did not want to understand.

Cory looked down at the floor from his bed in the dark stillness. It was darker in his room than usual. His nightlight had gone out and he could no longer see the clock on his nightstand. Not too long ago, he had been afraid of things under the bed. Needing to go to the bathroom had been a crisis of shameful fear.

Cory turned on his back and stared at the ceiling, wondering what, exactly, he had thought was under the bed those years ago. Definitely no tentacles. Probably something hairy.

As Cory mused, his ears started to pick up a barely audible rattling sound. Cory immediately went still to try to identify the faint noise. When he did, it got louder, clearly not imaginary. It progressed from a distant rattle to a shaky rumble, descending in octaves from fingernails on a wicker wall to a low growl.

Cory inhaled and the noise stopped. His body frozen, with adrenaline activated, Cory held his breath, staring at the ceiling. Only when he exhaled did the noise start again, this time much louder, much crisper, and plainly coming from under the bed. It was a growl, a deep guttural growl, so low that it vibrated the room.

Panic gripped Cory as he weighed screaming, leaping out of bed, or slapping himself. Was he dreaming? Was he hearing things? He had to see whatever was making this noise. If it wasn't real, he wouldn't be able to see it, right?

The growl stopped again. Cory crept to the edge of the bed and slowly peered over the lip to the floor below. Staring back at him, less than three feet away, was a black, grinning, red-eyed monster.

Its eyes shone brightly in the dark as Cory tried to comprehend what he was looking at. It was the head of a wolf, mounted on muscular humanoid shoulders, with big pointy ears too high on its head. It had pitch black, inch-long wiry fur, and a short, stubby snout. It was grinning ear-to-ear, displaying jagged, glistening teeth.

Cory's body went rigid as "I must be dreaming" repeated through his head. The monster chuckled a deep throaty laugh as two huge, three-clawed paws grabbed the bottom lip of the bed.

Slowly, Cory started to back away from the edge of the bed, but as he did, the monster pulled itself from under the bed and rose with him, keeping its gaze locked on Cory. Its eyes were tiny, bright pin pricks of red, and the longer Cory stared at them, the less real the rest of the Cory's vision seemed.

Shadows swirled behind the head of the thing as it rose to its full height, towering seven feet tall, still chuckling.

Cory tried with desperation to remember how he had handled the bad man. Having the bad man go away just made sense to him, it was the right thing to happen, it felt inevitable. But this creature made no sense. This monster had just manifested out of nothing, and it shouldn't even be able to fit under Cory's bed, out from which it crawled. This was a nightmare, not a bad man.

Cory's mouth began working in a whisper, "Dad… Dad…"

The monster filled the room with a loud snarl, bringing its claws up, and closing in towards Cory, who breathlessly repeated his call for help that built to a scream. "Dad…Dad…Dad!"

"Cory Nelson!" came Dad's angry voice from the doorway. Dad only used Cory's full name when he was doing something bad. Cory turned a quizzical look towards the door. The monster turned an identical expression towards Dad.

"You stop believing in that thing this instant!" Adam commanded Cory, pointing an accusing finger at the monster. Cory obeyed without thinking, instantly overcome by guilt. The monster disappeared with an audible "pop."

"That's better," said Adam. "Now, the power went out like we knew it eventually would, but that doesn't give you the right to stay awake playing with scary monsters, young man." Adam wagged his finger at Cory as he scolded. Adam's stern tone was tinged with a hint of humor. Cory was bewildered, but thankful that he wasn't actually in any trouble, either from monsters or from his Dad. He felt foolish for believing in his monster under the bed, and was relieved his Dad thought he was just playing, when in reality he had almost wet his bed.

"Sorry, Dad," Cory said with a sigh, pretending he really was just caught trying to stay up.

"Well, okay then. Have a good night Cory," Adam said as he turned and closed the door.

Adam shut Cory's door and leaned against it with a shaky shoulder. Claire watched expectantly with a flashlight in her hand.

"Well?" whispered Claire.

"It worked," sighed Adam. "I think we're good now. Cory is fine. It didn't even touch him." Adam's heart raced as he tried to process what he had just seen. Although he knew any monster that Cory conjured up was going to be scary, actually seeing a seven-foot-tall black beast standing in his house about to devour his son was nerve-wracking to say the least. Claire hugged him.

After a moment, Claire asked, "So what was it?"

"Oh, just your run-of-the-mill monster. Big teeth, red eyes," Adam shuddered again.

"Do you think you should still stay up and listen?" asked Claire. Adam had been spending the first few hours of every night sitting outside Cory's door, listening for any sound of monsters. Adam and Claire had discussed this strategy at length, and rather than tell Cory they were afraid of him creating a monster, they decided it would be best to catch him in the act to prevent him from doing it again.

"No, we should be good now," said Adam. "Cory made it disappear, so he knows he can do that now. I'm going to bed," said Adam, coming down off his own adrenaline. It was really a close call, considering the monster was seconds from attacking Cory, but Adam still felt it had been a better plan than the alternative. Admitting to Cory that his parents might not be able to stop a monster he created just seemed like the wrong approach.

Day 7

Sounds of screams filled the air as Jacob Christenson toured the destruction generated by his army. He had finally found a town worth destroying, a welcome respite from the miles and miles of boring Illinois farmlands.

Flanked by his two main men, Darrey and Mr. Chuckles, Jacob walked through the center of the town as fires burned out of control all around him. Jacob reached out to the nearest fire burning on the side of a building and spread it like butter up the wall. It was curious how the fire itself had no mass yet could still be manipulated like an object. Mannequins dressed in tuxedoes in a second story display window ignited and made Jacob return to the puzzle of what should be deemed valuable.

The government and police weren't a concern anymore, so cold hard cash was irrelevant. There was nothing, as far as Jacob could tell, that couldn't simply be taken with force alone, so why bother gathering trade goods? Carrying around gold and precious gems was equally pointless, as their only value was how prettily they sparkled. Why spend time looting when loot was worthless?

Women or slaves were also useless, since anyone still conscious was, by definition, armed and dangerous. Slaying was all well and good, but rape was nigh impossible. Jacob didn't need a rule against it; those who tried it typically got one or both of their heads torn off.

After much consideration, Jacob had decided that there really was only one thing of value in this new world: Men. Soldiers. Believers. Minds had always been a source of wealth, but now it seemed they were the only currency, the only way to measure both wealth and power.

Two of Jacob's men, one he recognized from Westvale, the other he did not, came running around the corner holding a third man by the arm.

"Colin Armando, offering new recruit named …" Colin said and elbowed the man he held by the arm.

"Uh, Robert Evans, uh … sir!" Robert said. His voice trembled, and Robert had blood on his arm.

"Robert!" cut in Jacob. Robert paled before Jacob.

Jacob proceeded with the speech. Inwardly, Jacob was weary of these words, and wished he had come up with something better that wasn't so cheesy. Outwardly, Jacob spoke with grave seriousness.

"Do you swear your mind, your soul, and your will to me, Jacob, to command as I see fit until such time as you are dismissed?" demanded Jacob, as he had done what felt like hundreds of times in the last few days.

This little oath of loyalty was something Jacob had designed to cement ties between himself and his new recruits. The "mind" part was for intellectuals, the "soul" part was for morons, and the whole thing was a promise that bound anyone who considered themselves honorable. A couple times, his men had brought him people who had shouted "no" to this question, at which point Jacob had focused his anger and disposed of the objectors in a mist of bloody disintegration. His men learned quickly not to bring Jacob unwilling subjects.

"Yes, sir, uh, I do sir," was the man's frightened yet hopeful response.

"Then Robert Whatever-the-hell-you-said-your-name-was, you are now part of the Brotherhood!" Upon saying this, Jacob reached out with his mind and shoved the newbie in the forehead, ever so slightly. He did this to seal the deal, for nobody liked their head pushed around, and this simple act always provoked a reflexive mental protest. This protest gave the new member a taste of the strength of Jacob's army behind his mind.

Robert stood still with wide eyes fixed on his new master as Jacob began walking away with his two lackeys in tow. Jacob tried not to think about Robert's thoughts. Robert didn't really consider himself a bad man, and wasn't fond of becoming a bad man, but it was obvious he was now on the winning team, and his gratitude was palpable. He had instantly gone from someone about to die to a member of what felt like the most powerful group of people on the planet.

The two who had brought Robert before Jacob cheered and gave hi-fives to the dazed newbie. "I told ya, man! Did you feel it?" one asked.

In contrast to Robert's elation, the whole scene irritated Jacob, not only because of how stupid the whole ritual was that he himself had devised, but also because Robert's mushy, pussy, sorry excuse for a mind made Jacob wonder if he should have torn Robert apart on the spot instead of welcoming him into the fold. The question of quality control in his new army weighed heavily on Jacob's mind. So far, it seemed quantity over quality was the best rule, but a platoon of pussies still felt like an unstable foundation.

Jacob didn't like the name he had come up with either. "The Brotherhood" was so damn cliché, but it was all he could think of at the time, considering Westvale was an all-male prison. It didn't make much sense when they started accepting a few badass chicks to the gang, but Jacob always had better things to worry about than branding.

Jacob continued walking through the middle of the town, looking for what he could designate as some sort of main base. Suddenly, he felt some men calling out for him. These cries were not audible; the men simply expected Jacob to hear their request.

Jacob bounded towards the request as his two men tried to keep up. Rounding a corner, he was confronted with a strange scene in an alley. Two of his men, Frisco and some other guy, were trying to approach a little girl, who couldn't be more than five or six years old. She had straight, brown hair and was clutching a Barbie doll, her eyes red with tears. She was sobbing slightly, but her eyes were also watching their every move.

"Shit," said Jacob. "I assume you've tried killing it?" Jacob queried.

Frisco backed away from the girl and turned towards Jacob, "Naw, but you know, Jacob, like… you sure we should?"

"Kids are fucking dangerous," stated Jacob. His worst battle losses had so far come from brats who had seen too many superhero movies.

Jacob held out his hand and began slowly approaching the girl.

"Hey now, we aren't all bad," cooed Jacob. As she watched Jacob approach, the little girl's crying raised a warning like an ambulance siren.

"No need for that, now, I'm not going to hurt you," Jacob said as he continued sauntering towards her.

The girl shrieked and everyone except Jacob was knocked to the ground by an invisible explosive wind. Jacob's hair did not move, nor was his slow approach disturbed. The girl had expected him to go flying like everyone else did when she screamed, but Jacob knew the rules no longer applied to him like she thought they should. She was a child; he was Jacob.

Jacob crouched in front of the wide-eyed girl, who was distracted trying to understand what Jacob was. He held his finger above her head and put his other hand on her shoulder.

"You see, we can be friends. I won't hurt you and you won't hurt us, right?" asked Jacob.

As the little girl paused to understand this offer, Jacob seized her head with his mind, which was focused on his finger. With his other hand, and with the strength of every man who promised their will to him, he spun the girl's body sideways with a sickening crunch.

Jacob released the girl as her dying mind tried to figure out what had just happened. Jacob stood, wiped his hands, and turned around towards his men, who were still getting up. Three of them wore expressions of shock. Darrey had a look of anger.

"What?" asked Jacob with a sly smile. Other people's emotions were always amusing.

"You didn't have to, you didn't. You. Fuck. Jesus Christ," stammered Darrey.

"No, sorry, but fuck you, Darrey. I absolutely had to do that. Kids are fucking dangerous, remember? Do you not remember Trent and Morgan? Or that poor bastard that had his head split open?" Jacob could list more of the Brotherhood slain by children in the last few days. Somehow, kids were capable of mental strength that had no place in Jacob's hierarchy.

Darrey turned and quietly stormed off. Jacob resumed his casual hunt for a new headquarters, this time only accompanied by Mr. Chuckles. He wanted a striking structure, either a museum or a government building that could be easily recognized, ideally one in the center of the town.

Jacob noticed Mr. Chuckles staring off in the distance. Jacob supposed normal people probably would be rattled after witnessing child murder. There was no question killing kids was bad for morale, but Jacob didn't see any other solution. The highest risk so far was likely encountering a kid too powerful for even Jacob to handle. Mr. Chuckles should get over it.

Rounding a corner, Jacob spotted some sort of town square. An ornate old building, designated as the hall of justice, sat facing the square, and it was exactly what Jacob was looking for.

Jacob set aside the buzzing inside his head and allowed himself to enjoy his discovery as he entered his new command center. He needed some time and some rest to regroup, to figure out his strategy and to plan his next move.

Outside the building was a plaque that informed Jacob of the name of the town he was busy destroying.

Bisby, founded 1864.

DAY 7

Things had been going smoothly at the church in Greenfield, so much so that people had started to make little trips back to their homes. Tom and Judy Bonner had been meaning to check on their place, and today they finally pulled into the driveway of their little house on their beet farm.

Judy stepped out of the truck and headed towards the door, but something caught Tom's eye.

"You go on ahead, hon. I need to check something first," said Tom.

"Sure. I'll be in the kitchen," smiled Judy. Judy had been excitedly planning to cook for the congregation and no doubt was full of amazing ideas.

Tom turned his attention towards JD, the stupid green tractor that defied all logic and stubbornly refused to start. Tom was going to get to the bottom of this puzzle once and for all.

Tom walked over to where the tractor was parked, unsure of how he was planning to tackle this issue, now with the power of a Tek on his side. He jostled the tractor with his mind for fun. It rocked in a cacophony of rusty metal.

He got up on the tractor and twisted the ignition. Nothing. "The damn thing just won't start," mumbled Tom.

But there was something. Tom felt a faint, confusing sensation of tension when he cranked the starter, similar to how the cross at the church had felt. It was as if someone was pushing on some cross that he was trying to hold down.

Tom turned the key again, feeling himself thinking about his own words. The damn thing won't start.

Tom paused for a moment. These were his words, but were they really true?

"This damn thing will too start!" Tom yelled angrily, and before he could finish the sentence, the tractor coughed out its own roar of life with a huge belch of black exhaust.

Stunned, Tom listened to JD rumble along happily. The culprit keeping JD from starting was obviously Thomas Bonner. Tom suddenly felt bad about how he had treated Greg the mechanic. Greg wasn't useless; he just couldn't start JD any more than Tom could because the problem wasn't mechanical. The problem was Tom.

Grinning, Tom stopped the tractor and walked back to his house.

As he opened the door, Tom was almost knocked over by the incredible blend of spices that assaulted his nose. Judy was at it again. Tom walked over to the kitchen to find Judy engaged in some kind of beautiful dance of pots, bowls, and spices, flying around her as she wore an ear-to-ear smile.

"I thought you were just going to grab some stuff for the church," said Tom with a smile.

"I couldn't help it!" answered Judy, beaming at Tom. "Just a quick lunch."

"Now Judy, don't get too crazy over there … we don't want to accidentally eat ourselves to death or anything," said Tom. Tom was only slightly kidding.

"Don't worry," said Judy, looking back towards Tom without so much as a pause in her prep work. "You're gonna love this."

Tom was sure of it.

DAY 7

Keith Pennison sat outside his apartment complex on the sidewalk on his sofa, watching the TV in front of him. He had decided he wanted to be outside and comfortable, so relocating his couch from his window was a relatively simple affair. It was drizzling slightly, but a large tarp hung in mid-air in a concave dome above his head, protecting his couch and his TV.

In the week since the Crack, Keith had come to learn a few things, primarily the disturbing lack of limits on anyone's power.

Keith held the end of the TV cord in one hand, the prongs of the plug facing the sky. The TV was on, streaming CNN, and Keith was trying to figure out how exactly this was happening. He knew he was doing it, that he had willed the TV to be playing without being plugged in, but he simply couldn't get a grip on the physics of the whole thing. There was clearly no current going through the wire. He flipped the prongs with his thumb without interrupting the broadcast. The only thing that made the TV sputter was when Keith doubted how the TV could possibly be turned on. Keith could follow the inert cord all the way down to the back of the TV, at which point if he kept tracing, the TV would flicker off. The point at which it would flicker off seemed dependent on where he thought the TV required electricity to function. The whole thing was so bizarre.

"…continue to return to their jobs, but now with extra abilities. Power grids are coming back online across the country as electric utility repair is no longer the hazardous, time-consuming…" CNN reported.

Keith's eye was distracted by something on the horizon, an orange streak zipping through the sky.

Someone else was flying.

Keith bounded up in an instant, strapping on his swimmer's goggles to protect his eyes from the wind. He wondered about his tarp + TV setup, but decided to just leave them. It didn't require any effort on his part to keep the tarp floating and the TV running, so he decided to test if they would still be standing when he got back.

Keith shot up from the sidewalk in hot pursuit of the orange streak, his loose clothes flapping in the wind. The orange dot was travelling north, across the city, and soon Keith could tell that it was a girl, dressed entirely in orange.

Keith's neck hurt. If you want to see where you are going, yet remain aerodynamic, you must hold your head up to look forward. A day of flying around holding your head up could really put a nasty kink in the neck.

Twenty feet away now, the girl turned around in mid-air and Keith got a good look at her. She was young, no more than 25 years of age, shapely, and was wearing a skin-tight orange spandex suit. She had sparkles on her face, red hair, and a huge smile.

Never mind the skin-tight suit, the girl's smile was her most striking feature. She wore a huge grin on her face even before she turned around, and she regarded Keith only with the mildest of interest. As she pivoted, it was obvious the girl didn't suffer from any kinks in the neck. Her movement was fluid and beautiful. Her eyes had a hint of Asian about them, but her skin's complexion, as well as her hypnotically flowing red hair, screamed American Irish.

Somehow, now that the orange streak was turned around and flying backwards, Keith always seemed to remain twenty feet away, no matter how fast or slowly he went. Keith tried to signal to the girl over the noise of the wind, flapping his arms, making speaking gesture with his hand, and pointing to the ground.

The girl only put her hand to her mouth, making a Japanese Schoolgirl giggle gesture of innocence. Keith realized she wasn't wearing any goggles.

Suddenly the girl was an orange blur flying circles around Keith. She had circled him ten times within a single second before Keith had time to react. Clearly, this girl had no respect for the laws of velocity and inertia, much less wind resistance. Keith began to wonder if the girl was even real, but he was afraid to make any attempt to touch her with his mind, lest she be angered.

The girl stopped her dizzying circles as suddenly as she had started, made an exaggerated yawn motion towards Keith, and then waved "bye-bye."

Keith knew what was about to happen and fought disappointment.

The girl turned, put her fist forward, and then, with an epic sonic boom, rocketed away from Keith to an orange pinpoint in the distance.

Deflated, Keith slowed and then floated gently to the ground. The girl was no longer visible. Keith still had a lot to learn. He was sad that he hadn't gotten to talk to the girl, but who knew if she even spoke English. That wasn't to say he hadn't learned something, something both disturbing and exhilarating.

In this new world, all bets were off.

DAY 7

"Nelsons?" came an unfamiliar voice echoing throughout the Nelson household. Claire looked up from their game of Mind Monopoly and gave her family a serious look to stay quiet.

The Nelson family had spent the last few days huddling together in the upstairs bedroom playing games and talking. Mind Monopoly was just Monopoly without using your hands, which wasn't really much more fun unless cheating was allowed. Pin the tail on the donkey was a favorite.

In many ways, this time had been very relaxing for Claire. Life had been so hectic for so long that this little forced vacation was actually kind of nice. The fact that little Cory was now the magical powerhouse of the family also left her feeling a little relieved.

"Hello, Nelsons?" the voice called again. The three of them stared at each other, frozen. Kessler had been their only contact with anyone outside the family since the nightmare had begun. It was Cory's turn, and the dice were floating in front of him. Claire motioned for Cory to drop them. She thought the voice sounded familiar.

"Nelson family? Are you in here?" came the voice again. This time Claire was sure she recognized the voice. She got up and cracked open the bedroom door, looking down the hallway towards the stairs for the source of the voice.

"Who is it?" Claire called, fairly confident that this was a neighbor.

"Claire? Is that you? Are you okay?" came the response.

Claire opened the door a little further and saw with relief that it was Lawrence picking carefully through the rubble of their living room. Lawrence chaired the neighborhood homeowner's association and lived down the block from the Nelsons. He had a clipboard in one hand.

"It's Lawrence," Claire called back to Adam, whose face showed no sign of recognition. "You remember, Lawrence Winston, from the HOA?" Adam continued to give her a blank look. "Honestly, Adam." Claire rolled her eyes and turned back to Lawrence.

"We're up here Lawrence! Come on up. Uh … be careful!" Claire meant for Lawrence to be careful as he made his way through the demolished downstairs, as well as to be careful not to cause any "incidents."

Lawrence hopped up the stairs to the doorway and took stock of the scene in the bedroom.

"Everyone okay?" Lawrence asked, giving Cory a suspicious look.

Adam and Cory, still seated around the monopoly board, nodded.

Lawrence addressed all of them. "Okay, here is the deal. Everyone still left in the neighborhood is gathering at the community center down on Oakwood."

Lawrence turned to Claire and said, "You know, where we have the homeowner meetings." Claire nodded. "One thing we know for sure is that there is safety in numbers, and if you are not part of a larger group, your chances of survival are significantly less." Claire and Adam had already been discussing earlier how they could find and join a group.

"There have been reports on the TV of large groups of bad people being very destructive, and the best thing to do is to group up yourself! So, Marsha, myself, and a few others decided our neighborhood should get together and be its own group. I figured, since the cars in our driveways show most of us are still here anyway, the folks on this block are as good a group as any. We have a generator running, too, as well as …"

Lawrence's speech faltered when a breeze turned his attention to the bedroom, where the sheet hanging on the wall covering the bloody crack billowed slightly. "Uh, what happened to you guys' door?"

Claire wasn't sure how to put it, but figured honesty was best. "Well, we had an intruder, who, uh, Cory was nice enough to take care of."

"You guys were lucky. Some haven't been …" Lawrence trailed off. He turned and smiled warmly at Cory. "I'll be sure to watch out for you, tough guy."

Embarrassed, Cory smiled and looked away. The adults in the room exchanged knowing glances.

"Anyway," Lawrence continued. "We have plenty of food and a generator, and best of all, we're all neighbors. You three really should come stay with us. You'll see why when you get there, everything just feels safe."

The Nelsons didn't really require any more convincing. Lawrence had them at "Nelsons." Everything about Lawrence's plan to move their residence into the community center with their neighbors was exactly what they were hoping for.

Lawrence scribbled something on his clipboard, started descending the stairs and bid them farewell.

"And don't drive. It's a short walk and we don't want to attract attention with a bunch of cars outside," Lawrence said as he picked through the ruins of the Nelson front door on his way to the next house.

All three threw together some clothes in a bag and set off for the community center. It was less than a mile away, so it would be easy to return if they forgot anything.

Arriving at the unassuming square building, the Nelsons were greeted with welcoming smiles by neighbors. Claire set about smiling and greeting, just as if she were attending a regular HOA meeting. Adam & Cory followed behind her.

Cory clung to his father's hand while Claire shouted greetings to neighbors whose names had been carefully memorized. Seeing the Terrell family, Claire paused, since the two wore hollow, distant stares. She didn't see the Terrell girl. Probably best not to ask. Claire nodded and continued.

"Claire, are you catching the looks?" came Adam's covert whisper behind her.

Claire had almost started to enjoy herself, but Adam was right: People kept giving Cory weird, sad looks and it was making Cory squirm. Claire realized that there should definitely be more children in the center.

"Nice to see you again, Mary" greeted Claire. Claire didn't like Mary Hammond much, since her son was not nice to Cory. Claire searched for Jeff and spotted him hanging out in front of the closet door. Right before Cory did.

Cory whirled about and locked eyes with Jeff Hammond, who was casually standing in front of a door, watching Cory with a smirk on his face.

"Hey Squeaks. Are you gonna squeak?" smiled Jeff.

Cory lost it.

"Don't! Call! Me!" Cory stated, taking big steps towards Jeff. "Squeaker!" yelled Cory bringing his hands in front of him and blasting Jeff through the door of the broom closet. Splintered remains of door and wall crashed all over the place as the adults in the room stood up, some grabbed their kids, others put their hands on their ears.

Jeff was laughing.

Jeff Hammond propped his head up from the floor to look at Cory, covered with dust and debris from the destroyed entrance to the closet.

"That all you got?" asked Jeff.

Cory paused in his advance, surprised but secretly relieved that he didn't actually do any damage to Jeff.

"Squeaker?" smiled Jeff.

"I'll fucking show you what I got!" yelled Cory as he jumped up to the destroyed wall, bringing his fists down on top of Jeff, invisible wrecking balls smashing Jeff further into the floor.

Cory could hear his parents meekly calling for him to stop, but they were just not important right now. Jeff was still laughing in his hole.

Jeff stood up, crawled out of his hole and smiled at Cory.

"Dude, Cory, we're superheroes. You can't hurt me," said Jeff. These words were ringing true to Cory's ears, and Jeff using his real name for once allowed his anger to fade. "Want to try?" asked Jeff, holding up his fist and smiling.

Realizing what was about to happen, Cory put his wrists to his face in a defensive posture, right before Jeff swung and blasted Cory into a brick wall, leaving a cartoonish outline of his body. The fact that Cory was as unhurt as Jeff made perfect sense to both of them.

"That's enough you two!" shouted Claire above the noise. "We have to live here, for God's sake, don't wreck the place!"

Cory stepped back through the wall and obeyed his mother, exchanging a sheepish grin with Jeff.

DAY 10

It was around two o'clock in the morning inside the Bisby Judicial Hall where Jacob Christenson slept in the judge's chambers off the courtroom.

Suddenly Jacob awoke with a start. His body was under attack.

A quick check of the room showed nothing amiss, and he could tell that the guard outside in the hallway did not sense anything.

It came again.

Voodoo. A poppet. Someone was trying to stab Jacob with a pin using a voodoo doll. That someone was being unsuccessful, and that someone was starting to panic.

Jacob jumped straight through the window with a crash, fell two stories and landed in an alley, cracking the pavement with his shoes. Straightening, he got a location on this soon-to-be-in-horrible-pain medicine man. The wannabe shaman was less than a mile away, still in Bisby, and Jacob shot off like a rocket to meet him.

When he arrived at the small, old, rundown house surrounded by larger buildings, Jacob blew the door open and strode inside. As he did, the head of a short, white guy turned to him. He was in the process of repeatedly hitting a voodoo doll with a hammer. The doll was unharmed. This guy's name was Lyle.

"Why the fuck aren't you dead!?" screamed the frustrated Lyle, tears streaming down his face. At the same time, Lyle threw the hammer at Jacob's head.

Jacob allowed the hammer to hit in response to Lyle's question. The hammer bounced harmlessly off of Jacob's forehead.

"Don't you know?" cooed Jacob. "My skin is like mithril, my bones are like adamantium. You don't happen to know how to harm imaginary metals, do you?"

Lyle picked up the poppet, frantically trying to twist it in his hands.

"Nice try," said Jacob, as he took the doll from Lyle.

The battle was won by the time he walked through Lyle's door. Lyle's whole plan was to kill Jacob from afar, and Lyle wholeheartedly believed that if he failed, his death would be certain.

"You fool," said Jacob, as he seized Lyle's skeletal structure. "You still believe in me, even now." It was almost harder for Jacob *not* to kill Lyle.

As Jacob clenched his fist and crumpled Lyle's body like a piece of paper, he turned his attention to the poppet. This whole voodoo thing was new and interesting.

Jacob quizzically tugged at the doll's arm and tried to twist it but felt his own beliefs about his indestructible body preventing him from being able to damage the doll. This seemed very strange to Jacob, since the person who believed in the voodoo was dead. How could this doll still affect him?

Jacob tried to believe that the doll was not linked to him, but his attention was immediately drawn to the little piece of hair attached to the top of the poppet. Jacob tried again, saying out loud, "this doll is not linked to me."

Immediately Jacob felt resistance from something very strong and very old, believed in by millions of people. Voodoo. Jacob's eyes widened as his own words registered as false to his ears. The belief in the magic of voodoo itself was something that Jacob was not capable of disbelieving. It didn't seem to matter that Jacob knew the very idea of the Voodoo Doll was almost purely Hollywood garbage, with nothing to do with the actual Haitian Voodoo beliefs.

Jacob removed the hair, and immediately the doll could be crumpled in his hand. This was an interesting development. Caution should be taken when confronting shared or religious beliefs.

As Jacob walked back to his headquarters in the night, he firmly confirmed the belief that he was no longer going to be shedding any of his hairs.

Day 10

Keith landed gently beside a Volvo that looked abandoned on an onramp to I-90 in Seattle. He opened the door and stepped into the passenger seat. Having spotted from above a few cars still making their way on the freeways, and since he had once again failed to find any wrongs that needed righting today, Keith decided to experiment again.

The explanation given to Freeway Fear as a phenomenon never really sat right with Keith. Though it was clear that everyone on the planet was now an overpowered Tek, it was still a mystery exactly why driving down the highway gave people the heebie-jeebies. His early experiment with the cab ride over I-90 had only left him with more questions. His new plan was to find another car on the road and then try to take the driving attitude of a defensive and then an aggressive driver, to see if he could pinpoint the origin of the feelings they generated.

Lacking any normal method to make the car go, Keith simply willed the car to start. Keith felt a minor protest from old physics about the key not being present.

Keith willed the car forward, or rather, he believed the car should go forward. As the acceleration pushed him to the back of his chair, he was once again struck by the amazing lack of effort this took. Having spent weeks struggling with mental effort to make things move, the half-thought it now took to accelerate a two-ton hunk of metal to freeway speeds was still surprising. He wondered how David Archer had progressed in the pre-Crack times.

His self-propelled Volvo entered onto the I-90 freeway, heading across Lake Washington once again.

The bridge was in relatively good repair, having been spared any major damage. After worrying for a minute that he wouldn't find any subjects for his research, Keith noticed a blue Dodge Challenger appear in his rear-view mirror, closing in on him fast. Keith carefully prepared his thoughts and decelerated.

The dodge drove up beside him, and the driver showed himself as a husky white guy dressed in black with about an inch of hair covering his little round head.

"Hey, I'm Zach. Wanna race?" asked the hot-rodder, grinning cheerfully.

Keith jumped into the driver seat, confident in his own mental abilities, sure that Dodge vs. Volvo was going to be way more about Zach vs. Keith.

"It's Keith, and absolutely," Keith fired back with an eager smile. Playfulness should be the default attitude of the new world.

"Okay, I'll count it off, you ready?" queried Zach.

"Yup!" answered Keith, gunning his little engine with his mind for effect.

"On your marks, get set, go!"

The wheels of Keith's Volvo spun, smoked, and peeled out in a perfect image of every street race Keith had ever seen on TV. The Challenger, on the other hand, did not lose traction for an instant, and was immediately far out in front of Keith.

As his car picked up speed, Keith realized he was going to lose. He expected his wheels to spin faster than his opponent's, but he instead should have expected that his car would race down the highway faster. Keith pictured himself catching up, and closed the gap quickly, possibly because his opponent also wanted him to catch up. Soon Keith was right on Zach's tail.

Keith could feel Zach's will. Zach wanted him to stay behind, and Keith could tell that Zach could tell that Keith wished to pass him. It was high speed, electric tug-of-war, and the only thing they both agreed on was that it was unsafe to push much faster than 100 mph.

The freeway curved through a tunnel to the right and both cars shot around the corner. Immediately both drivers were surprised to discover another abandoned car parked sideways in the middle of the road, across both lanes. In a single fluid motion, Keith pulled his car up on its two right wheels to avoid it, and the Dodge pulled itself up onto its two left wheels. The racing cars flew by the obstruction and returned, crashing, to the freeway, both still going around 100.

Keith and Zach regained their composure, both minds checking on the other's safety, and then the race was back on, two thrilled drivers locked in a battle of wills.

Keith remembered his joyride's scientific origins, and tried to imagine what a timid, defensive driver would feel about the situation. A defensive driver would drive by reaction, turn when their signpost came up, brake if the car in front of them got too close. Immediately, Zach's will overwhelmed Keith, and instantly, Zach shot out way ahead of Keith.

Quickly, before he lost the race, Keith decided to switch to the other kind of driver. Keith filled his mind with aggression. He saw his path, his turns were planned, and he chose his lane intentionally. In this mindset, Keith was the angry winner of this race.

Protests from Zach about this fact were sharply rebuffed in Keith's mind, and very quickly, Keith's little car had shot past Zach's, going well over 200 mph. Zach tried to believe he was faster, that he was a winner, but Keith had locked down the future in which the Volvo beats the Dodge.

The race was over, and Keith was the victor, there was no question about this fact. Keith pulled off in a turnabout, while Zach's Dodge lifted straight off the road, spun 180 degrees, landed on the westbound lane, and headed back to Lake Washington, presumably in search of another competitor.

The Freeway Fear finally made sense. It was a battle of wills on the freeway, where neither of the combatants realized that they were in a battle at all.

A strange thought crossed Keith's mind. I-90 seemed weirdly longer, and the amount of time spent driving on it should have taken them further than he was from the lake. It was probably just his imagination, but Keith momentarily wondered exactly how much of reality was relative to belief.

Day 11

"Hey Cory, I wanna show you something," was Jeff Hammond's exciting invitation. Cory quickly looked up to his mother, seated on the cot next to him at the community center, and bolted away the moment her eyes drifted away in assent.

Cory Nelson and Jeff Hammond, once mortal enemies, had somehow become best friends, much to everyone's surprise. They were the only kids close to each other's age in the center and had started hanging out for lack of alternatives.

But that didn't mean Cory trusted Jeff.

"Am I going to like it?" ventured Cory, following Jeff through main doors of the meeting hall and into the foyer.

"Totally," smiled Jeff, leading Cory outside.

Cory realized he didn't need to question Jeff's honesty anymore, since if Jeff was lying, Cory would feel it immediately. Believing he would "totally" enjoy Jeff's surprise didn't raise any conflicts, so Jeff must believe that too. Sometimes, Cory kind of liked this new world.

Jeff led Cory outside and around the back of the recreation center. They rounded the corner and Jeff held out his hand for Cory to stay back.

"You don't want to spook him," said Jeff.

Him? thought Cory.

As Cory watched, a strange, four-legged, bird-like creature stepped out from behind the dumpster. It was a griffin. Its body was about chest-high to Cory, with a white eagle-ish head and a smooth, shiny green body. Powerful-looking paws gripped the gravel and its wings were tucked neatly at its sides.

"That's not real!" exclaimed Cory, after which the creature turned and vanished behind the dumpster. As it did so, Cory was keenly aware of Jeff's disagreement with his statement.

"Of course he isn't, but check it out—he can be," replied Jeff. "Griff there is very loyal and friendly, and he can even fly you around if you want him to."

"Griff?" said Cory, slowly allowing himself to believe in whatever it was that Jeff was pushing. Slowly, the griffin poked its head out from around the corner, and nervously approached them again, eyeballing Cory. Cory smiled. Griff's eyes looked like Jeff's.

"Go ahead, pet him, Squeaks," said Jeff.

Angered by the mention of his old nickname, but deciding to let it slide, Cory reached out and felt the bird-lion's head. Its green head felt like fine feathers, but he also felt Jeff's mind when he touched it. It obviously felt like feathers because Jeff believed it should feel like feathers. Also, he didn't really like touching Jeff's mind.

"Cool," stated Cory.

"Griff is great. He can't talk or anything, but you can always tell what he's thinking," said Jeff affectionately as he scratched Griff's head. Cory suspected Jeff's relationship with Griff existed before Griff himself existed. Then he had another thought.

"So, you need him to fly?" asked Cory.

"Well, uh, they said it was bad to try to grab yourself," stammered Jeff.

Jeff waved his hand and Griff winked out of existence as he turned towards Cory.

"Naw, you don't grab yourself, you just do it … watch," said Cory. At the end of his sentence, he began to levitate up into the air.

Jeff fidgeted a bit while watching him before asking, "So you're not grabbing yourself? What are you doing then?"

"Dumbass! That's the trick—you don't try to do anything, you just fly! Do it, Jeff!" yelled Cory, as he started to make a circle around Jeff about ten feet above him.

Jeff closed his eyes and inhaled deeply, stuck his arms straight out and moved vertically. About five feet up, Jeff opened his eyes, wobbled, tilted, and spun out of control, crashing back to the ground.

Cory couldn't help but laugh his ass off.

"Ow! It's not funny, Squeaker!!" But even his hated nickname couldn't stop Cory from laughing.

"Why does it even have to hurt, dumbass?" Cory was near tears, floating around in a ball, laughing hysterically.

Jeff smiled and stood up, getting ready to try again. Cory knew he was right. And he knew Jeff's fat ass had stopped hurting.

Day 14

Jacob Christenson led his army to battle through the west exit of the town of Bisby. This time it was some biker group, Hell's Angels or some such nonsense, that had formed with a leader that was challenging Jacob's authority.

Jacob had taken about fifty loyal men with him, all of whom could be counted on. As the Brotherhood had expanded, Jacob had decided he needed to assign ranks to keep everyone in line. These men were rank two, who enjoyed the privilege of accompanying him on raids and battles.

He had brought Darrey with them, even though he continued to fail to understand the necessity of killing kids. Jacob still wondered how Darrey could object if he had no logical alternative.

The Brotherhood closed in on the biker gang, who was obviously ready for them. About fifteen men stood in the street, also in a triangle formation. They were dressed in leather and denim, with stern expressions and fixed jaws. It was clear they lacked the proper fear, and it was clear they had their own champion, a graying man standing at the front of the V and matching Jacob's stare.

Jacob smiled as he approached. It was rare to find an organized, confident group such as this. This should be fun.

The man made the first move, which was fine with Jacob, as he remained focused on the woeful mistake this group was making.

"The Sons of Silence have no quarrel with you," stated the man as Jacob's army was about thirty feet away. Jacob disagreed with this statement to see what he was up against.

Bruce Reed's mind felt damaged. He had some sort of harsh past that made his thoughts strong. He also clearly felt that his little biker gang was something special, and that it was incredibly strong at his command.

"I'm afraid the Brotherhood does have a quarrel with you," answered Jacob, realizing he should have prepared better retorts. But this statement did the job, since both men could tell it was true.

"Is that so?" asked Bruce. "Are you just looking for a fight, then?"

Jacob could tell the man was baiting him, trying to get him to go along with his truth.

"Not at all," said Jacob. "All you and your men need to do is to join the Brotherhood" he smiled. "You guys look like you'd fit right in."

This elicited a different reaction from the Sons of Silence. There were shadows of smiles, smirks here and there, and a furrowed brow or two of dissension. Jacob had struck a nerve, and Bruce didn't like it.

"Unlike you, we still have our honor," said Bruce, with obvious hesitation. Who the hell could define "honor" anyway?

"Then you can die!" Jacob cut in, picturing his hand grabbing Bruce's heart and squeezing. Too late and too slow, Bruce realized believing in impervious skin was not sufficient protection.

Bruce Reed doubled over with gurgle, much to the astonishment of the Sons of Silence. As was standard procedure, Jacob's men roared and charged, but also according to standard procedure, Jacob raised his hand and they all froze in mid-air, with sadistic smiles on their faces.

"I see strength in all of you," said Jacob, addressing the biker gang, all still trying to comprehend how they had just lost their leader, a friend, the battle, and were about to lose their lives, all in a matter of seconds. "You have a choice. Join the Brotherhood. Or die."

Most of the Sons of Silence stood still, but a few turned and ran. Jacob lowered his hand and his army resumed its charge, this time only after the men who were trying to flee.

Jacob tried to sense where the cowards believed they would be safe from him and picked up something about a church group in the forest.

The rest of the new recruits needed initiation. Jacob sighed and got to work.

Day 17

Tom and Judy sat in a circle on little plastic chairs in the downstairs rec room of the Meadowview Methodist church. Edgar and Carlos were with them, along with two other couples.

They were drinking wine.

"Dis is good shit," smiled Carlos, showing purple teeth after drinking from his blue plastic cup. His accent was back to being barely noticeable.

"Ain't it?" smiled Tom. "Never thought I'd turn into a wino, but I ain't never thought a lot of things lately."

Judy passed the jug to her friend Carol after refilling her cup.

"I don't remember any scripture about turning water into beer," she giggled.

"Also," said Tom, "wasn't it only Jesus who could turn water to wine? How the hell did Jim Bailey do it? Is he Jesus now?" Tom's joke sent a ripple of laughter through the group.

"Hay man, don't be askin' questions," smirked Edgar. "Just keep dem jugs coming."

"Really makes you think, doesn't it?" mused Judy.

Tom turned to his wife, whose cheeks had quickly assumed a rosy tinge.

"About what?" asked Tom, concerned Judy was about to wreck the festive mood.

"Well, I mean, do you all remember your Exodus?" she asked.

"Aw yeah," said Carlos. "Moses and dem all?"

"Right. I mean, if Bailey could turn water to wine with our little flock, imagine if he had six hundred thousand faithful Israelites at his back," stated Judy. The old bible story didn't sound quite so fanciful anymore.

A man named Peter Hutchinson looked sullenly into his glass. He seemed to be the only one not enjoying himself.

"Hey so what's eating you, Peter? Are you not liking happy hour?" asked Tom, changing the subject.

Peter took a moment before looking up at them.

"Did you all hear about Bisby?" he asked quietly.

The group exchanged blank looks. Peter's wife looked away.

"What about Bisby?" Tom asked.

"Destroyed. Gone. I heard everyone there is either dead or ran away," said Peter.

Edgar sipped his cup in the awkward silence that followed.

"How?" asked Tom, regretting having brought up the subject.

"Some bad group. A prison group, they said. Apparently, this gang of thugs has been running all over the place, killing people and taking whatever they want."

"Do you think they would ever come here?" asked Judy, expressing the question on all their minds.

"Bisby's not that far away," said Peter.

"Dona suppose Mr. Bailey would protect us," said Edgar halfheartedly.

"Well, I for one, know he would put up a fight," said Judy reassuringly.

"Do you think we should leave?" asked Tom.

"And go where?" asked Judy, shooting Tom an angry look. "I'm sorry, but did I miss some larger, stronger, safer group somewhere? Meadowview church is as good a place as any, and besides, don't we owe our support to Bailey?"

The group turned their eyes away from Judy. She rarely got so fired up.

"Relax. We ain't goin nowhere," said Carlos.

Carlos was right. There was no Plan B.

"Sorry, hon," said Tom. "Of course we got the reverend's back," as he reached out his hand and the jug of wine floated over to him.

"Careful, don't spill" said Judy.

"C'mon, I ain't that useless," said Tom. Judy was back to smiling.

Happy hour continued as normal, interspersed with speculation on what would happen if the prison group that destroyed Bisby came to Meadowview.

DAY 19

Claire Nelson picked up her clipboard and set off to make her rounds at the community center. She was happy Lawrence had given her one of the rare jobs available.

Cory and Jeff were almost always MIA lately, usually flying around somewhere, trying out some fantastical power or another. Claire couldn't help but worry, especially since she wasn't sure Jeff was such a great influence on Cory. At the same time, Cory's seemingly effortless transition to this new world made her and Adam feel like afterthoughts.

Sometimes Adam would accompany her, but today he was talking to his friend Jared, so Claire decided not to interrupt.

First stop was new arrivals, but today there were none. Yesterday, Old Man Murphy had shown up, so Claire decided to go check on him.

"Good morning, beautiful!" beamed the 80-year-old as Claire approached. She was slightly taken aback, but happy he was not his usual grouchy self. Kids avoided Old Man Murphy's house, and Claire wasn't sure she had ever seen the old curmudgeon smile.

"Well, hello there, Mr. Murphy. You seem to be in a good mood," was Claire's understatement.

"Hah! How can I not be? Remember that excruciating arthritis pain I had for oh, twenty-odd years? That's right, you don't–'cause you never asked. Well guess what? It's gone, and I feel like a million bucks! Ha haw!" exclaimed Mr. Murphy as he danced a little jig on the floor.

"You go girl!" called Jeannette at the old man. Smiles were everywhere.

"Okay, I'll mark you down as 'acclimated,'" said Claire, scribbling in her book and smiling at the festive mood of the room. The elderly always seemed to be in good spirits lately. It seemed the more wrinkles you had before the Crack, the more smiles you wore after it.

Claire headed to the storeroom after checking on a few more families. Not everyone had smiles; in fact, some faces still wore signs of trauma, especially those who had lost children.

Arriving at the storeroom, Claire checked her notes against the inventory and confirmed the continuation of a trend: People weren't eating.

There were the same number of survival buckets of MREs. The same number of canned peas, beans, and fruit. Really, the only thing they had ran out of was coffee, and some residents had started bringing in their own Keurig supplies for that.

When Lawrence had first tasked her with inventory, he was extremely worried that the number of people at the community center would chew through their entire supply of food in less than a week, maybe two. But consumption had slowed, and at this rate, their supplies might last months. Claire wondered if people really needed to eat anymore.

Claire caught sight of herself in a mirror hanging on the storeroom door. She looked good. In fact, she thought everyone at the center was looking good. The fat seemed less fat, the skinny were looking meatier, faces were more symmetrical, and everyone seemed to have fewer wrinkle lines.

Claire wondered if humanity could still be considered human.

DAY 20

Jacob Christenson drove his murder bus through the forest. He had torn the top half of the bus off, so jagged pieces of windows and twisted metal lined the sides. It was late at night, and although he could barely see the road, staying on the windy forest road took minimal effort.

Jacob had a lot on his mind. Although he had arranged this little expedition to the church with those who deserved a reward and wanted a little fun, there was more than one reason for this trip.

The most interesting reason was that Jacob felt pulled towards the church. It was as if the members inside the church desired to be destroyed by a scary group. Jacob was happy to oblige.

The other reason was that rumors were that this was a "good" group. As if Jacob's group was somehow "bad." As if his men didn't have a great time doing whatever the hell they wanted. He hadn't run across any group not ruled by fear, and he didn't need his men getting the idea that a "good" group was somehow superior to theirs. The churchies had to go.

Jacob also had started feeling like he needed a vacation. He had succeeded in amassing so many minions that he was starting to wonder what the purpose was of such a giant army. The administration duties alone were giving him a headache. He needed to delegate more.

"So, what, are you going to just kill them all too?" asked Darrey, seated behind Jacob. He had gotten so mouthy recently.

"If I have to, which I probably will," answered Jacob. "And I don't like your tone," he added. Such insolence from anyone else might have needed a stronger response. But Darrey had always been a good sounding board, and usually knew when it was the right time to talk.

Darrey looked pouty but shut his face. He had to know Jacob was right.

The mangled bus slowed and entered the driveway of the Meadowview church. As his men roused and fanned out from the bus, Jacob's attention was immediately drawn to the wooden cross hanging atop the building. There were minds attached to it.

"Fascinating," said Jacob. He could feel the minds of the farm people just by caressing the cross. Jacob pushed gently on the cross with his mind, and felt the entire congregate, led by a man named Bailey. Jacob's little push announced his presence, and the churchfolk's rising fear forced a smile to Jacob's lips.

"Incredibly stupid, but fascinating," said Jacob as Mr. Chuckles burst out laughing. Their shit-dumb holy man had permanently given away all their positions. All he needed to do to track them is to see who still believed that cross wouldn't move.

The door to the church opened as Jacob approached. Outside stepped a single man wearing a clergy collar. This must be their leader, Bailey.

Jacob put his hand up to his face. Bailey had just separated himself from view of his supporters. This separation was the goal of several of Jacob's battle tactics, and the fucking retarded holy man had just done it for him. Bailey had probably never fought anyone before.

"Who dares defy this house of the Lord?" was the reverend's comical attempt at courage. Jacob barely let the man finish his sentence and cut in with his reply.

"I do! I am Jacob, and you will call me Lord, or else you will die. All of you." Jacob was pleased with his snappy retort, and it did the trick. Ripples of fear came from inside the church from those who could hear him.

"We will not … I say!" stammered the reverend.

In a quiet voice, and only loud enough so the reverend could hear, Jacob said, "oh yeah, you've got to go," and imagined a fireball being blown across the reverend's entire body.

Fire coalesced in front of the reverend, billowy and ball shaped. As it slowly advanced on the preacher, Bailey put his hands up and parted the flames, creating a bubble of air around him as the flames passed over him. A glimmer of hope flashed on Bailey's face.

Unfortunately for Bailey, Jacob's fireball was a trap. He just wanted to get the leader on the same page, which is why he imagined his fireball as weak and slow. This was the jab before the uppercut.

"Gotcha," said Jacob quietly, as he felt Bailey's realization that he had just been allowed to part Jacob's fireball.

"Goodbye," said Jacob as he clenched his fists and imagined white hot lightning coursing through Bailey's body. This time, there was no way out for the enemy.

Bailey's mind collided with Jacob's mind, and Jacob became instantly aware of Jim Bailey's doubts about his own sermons. This man was not so much a man of faith as a man of believing in goodness. He believed in himself only as much as he believed in the power of good.

Jacob on the other hand, had no doubts about himself. Jacob had understood the value of believing in himself many years before the Crack.

Bailey's hesitant confidence was no match for Jacob's sharpened certainty. The last thing reverend Bailey thought was that Jacob was right, he was a piece of inconsequential dust compared to this powerful nightmare of a man.

Electricity flared through the reverend's body, electric arcs multiplying and expanding. In less than a few seconds, Jacob released his fists and the electricity stopped. The stiff, blackened, and smoky body of Jim Bailey fell to the ground.

The leader disposed of, several top members of Jacob's gang, who had been waiting in formation behind him, began rushing the church.

"Kill them all!" was Jacob's triumphant and blood-curdling command to his gang. The truth of this statement was that he didn't really need the churchgoers eradicated, the simple disbanding of the organized group was really all he came for. But trying to recruit from these goody-goodies was surely more trouble than it would be worth, as he already regretted recruiting a few pussy-foot excuses for soldiers.

Day 20

"Dammit, Judy, you know full well as I do that Reverend Bailey ain't got a chance in hell of standing against that man out there," hissed Tom. They were in the back of the church, next to the rear exit. "Everyone in this place knows it, but we are the ones next to the door, so we are the ones who have to do something about it!" Tom tried to keep his voice down, but he knew he had already attracted the attention of Edgar and several others in the congregation. Fight or flight was on everyone's minds.

"But if we run, everyone will run!" Judy whispered under her breath back at Tom.

"But that's their choice, Judy, and by the way, they should run, and so should we! Don't try to tell me we shouldn't. You know we should!"

"But what about Bailey?" asked Judy, almost to tears.

"He should have ran too, as far as I'm concerned," Tom didn't like it, but Judy had a point. Did they owe the reverend their support? He was, after all, the one who brought them together in the first place.

"Kill them all!" came an evil voice from outside the church. Bailey was dead. The shock of knowing this fact caused panic. Edgar shoved his way past Tom and Judy through the exit.

In an instant, the walls of the church blew open, exposing the congregation to the darkness. Churchgoers scattered as Tom and Judy ran through the back door and into the woods. A sinister laugh, echoing through the dark woods and mixed with screams, faded into the background as Tom tried to keep up with Judy.

After about ten minutes of jogging, Judy finally stopped to catch her breath. Tom and Judy panted together in the darkness as some ominous noises came from the direction of the church.

Then they felt it again. His name was Jacob, and he had just shoved the cross on the top of the church. He knew where they were. Jacob knew where they all were.

Tom and Judy started running again, this time in a slightly different direction, but still away from the church. After another five minutes, Judy stopped again and turned breathlessly to Tom.

"What do we do, Tom? I'm scared …" sobbed Judy.

"I know, I know," Tom said between breaths, "But keep it together, hon, we're going to get through this."

"How, Tom? How do we fight a man like that? You felt him just like I did, you saw what he did, what do we do?" cried Judy, wringing her hands in front of her.

"Well, I don't know, Judy," Tom retorted with a tinge of anger in his voice. Despair never failed to irritate him. "In fact, I don't know much of anything right now, but let me tell me what I do know: Going to pieces ain't going to help anything."

Judy sobbed quietly for a moment as she tried to regain her composure. Poor Judy hardly ever lost control.

"Now let's just look at this logically, there must be a solution," Tom said, unsure of whether he was telling the truth. Judy continued sulking, but she was listening.

"From the feel of it, I would bet that Jacob guy is going to be able to find us, so running forever ain't gonna work. We're gonna have to fight him, one way or the other.

"Now ol' Bailey was a good guy, but you and I both knew he had no balls, which I think is pretty important these days."

Judy wiped a few tears and frowned at Tom, but said nothing.

"I sure ain't going to be crossin horns with no Jacob, but there's got to be someone who has big enough balls for the job. All we really need is a good guy with some big balls, that's all," concluded Tom.

"Oh right Tom, so how do we find this superman, out here in the deep woods of Illinois?" Judy asked, cynically.

Tom thought for a minute. The answer was staring him in the face.

"We pray," Tom stated.

"Pray?" Judy stared skeptically at Tom. "Thomas Bonner, who do you think you are fooling? I know full well you ain't much of a Christian."

"That doesn't matter!" Tom went on, excitedly. "Think about it, what do you do when you pray? You believe your prayers will be answered, that's what."

"So, you want to kneel down here and pray for someone to rescue us?" asked Judy.

"Yup," said Tom, kneeling and pulling Judy down to the forest floor with him. "We are going to kneel right here, and we are going to pray for someone, someone good and someone strong. This someone will be stronger than Jacob, and this someone will save us. We are going to pray like our lives depend on it, cause they do."

Judy knelt next to her husband with her hands folded in front of her while Tom prayed with all his might. Dawn approached as the two kneeled in silence, believing in a miracle with all their hearts.

Day 20

Keith had been doing a lot of thinking.

It was late at night, probably close to 3am, and Keith was strolling through Mercer Slough park by moonlight. He had decided his hoodie would always keep him warm and he had decided the moon would let him see perfectly. The experience was amazingly pleasant and added a whole new dimension to his favorite park. The place sounded much more alive than during daylight hours, and even things not touched by moonlight glowed as if they were. But Keith's mind was elsewhere.

Keith was wondering again about a question that had been on his mind many years before any weirdness ever appeared in the world, a question that just about every person on the planet grapples with at some point: What was his purpose in life?

Before this whole mess started, Keith remembered feeling a little purposeless, but it wasn't something that bothered him much. He never considered himself really "special," in the sense that he was never in a position to take on the world's problems. He had been content trying to do good in his little life, making a small difference by trying to make life more pleasant for those around him. But in the weeks leading up to the telekinetic disaster, Keith had started feeling like he was "meant" for something greater, that he was a superhero in disguise.

Then came the Crack, and it seemed like his skills were very much in demand. But then after a day or two, the world seemed to settle down rather quickly, and it seemed like his skills were suddenly not needed anymore. Was he really back to a purposeless existence?

Keith realized now that he had been hoping this philosophical question was going to be answered by someone else, and he had probably been hoping this ever since he was able to ask the question. Growing up in a stubbornly atheist family, Keith had always looked down on those who chose the easy path of religion to provide answers to life's philosophical and spiritual questions.

But Keith realized he was tired of wrestling with them by himself. Just because he didn't believe in organized religion didn't mean he was above asking for help. He needed someone who knew more than he did. He needed a Rupert.

Keith paused his stroll. Why not Rupert?

"Rupert?" Keith said out loud. The crickets ignored him.

Keith knew he should be able to talk to Rupert, but waiting for something to happen was the wrong approach. He needed some sort of Facetime, but the likelihood of Rupert possessing a working phone was close to nil. Plus, such technology really should not be necessary anymore.

Keith walked over to a particularly calm eddy of water next to the stream and looked down into it. Rupert was going to appear in it. Keith focused his beliefs on this idea.

In a few seconds, the water shimmered then cleared, showing what looked like a brick wall. Keith turned his head trying to figure out what he was looking at. The wall was dark and dirty, and looked like it had a bunch of chewed gum stuck to it. Possibly downtown?

Something green flashed in front of the wall and the image rippled.

"Rupert?" asked Keith.

"Who said that?" came Rupert's voice as the image of the wall steadied again.

"It's me, Keith. Are you there?" Keith couldn't help but smile at the sound of Rupert's voice.

"I am here. Where are you?" asked Rupert, as his face came into the frame. Keith mostly saw his chin, as he was searching around for the sound of Keith's voice.

"Look down," said Keith. Rupert turned his face down. He looked different. First of all, he was clean, but he had also apparently traded his dirty rags for a proper Mad Hatter costume. He wore a big green hat with a 10/6 on it and an outrageous monocle that mysteriously stayed fastened over his right eye.

"Well, hello there Keith! What are you doing in a puddle?" asked Rupert.

"Trying to talk to you, of course!" said Keith.

"Well, mission accomplished, boy! But I'm a very busy man, you know," Rupert said as he glanced around. "People to be, things to see, stuff to most definitely not do."

Keith always barely knew what Rupert was talking about but decided he should make it quick.

"So, what now? What are the rules of this new world?" asked Keith.

"Oh, you know," said Rupert as he looked around distractedly. "Belief is real, two is greater than one, circle takes the squares."

"Circle? What? Tic-tac-toe?" asked Keith.

"Hah! Yahtzee!" exclaimed Rupert. "No, no. You're a circle, my boy. You take all the squares!" Rupert looked away, grinned and pointed at something Keith couldn't see.

"I gotta go, Keith. Like I said, sights to feel!" said Rupert.

"Wait, just one more question," pleaded Keith. "What should my purpose be?"

"Hah! Idiot boy! It's whatever you want it to be! Obviously!" and with that, Rupert was gone in a flash of green.

Keith stood up and continued walking down the path in the park by the moonlight.

Keith liked the idea of being a superhero, and he liked the idea of helping people. If he wanted this to be his purpose, he just had to believe it was his purpose. Obviously.

So, he wanted to go where he was needed. No, that wasn't quite right, he should just try to believe that he was going where he was needed. And if he wanted to intervene in a conflict where he could make a difference, he should just believe he was about to intervene in exactly such a conflict.

This concept thrilled Keith, and he found himself quickening his pace. Since the Crack, no other experiment of his had failed, so most likely this one would work, too. Keith corrected himself. This one would work too.

Keith knew that he had to be careful. He had seen some pretty horrible things on the internet, and definitely didn't want to find himself on the receiving end of someone's unfathomable wrath. He shuddered to think of what happened when that flying orange chick got mad. Keith wanted to stop what he could stop, not attempt to stop what he might not be able to stop. But he also wanted to make a difference. The little group of businesspeople he had "rescued" from their druggie antagonist Lester right after the Crack had barely needed rescuing. That whole situation probably would have resolved itself if he hadn't intervened.

Keith kept getting distracted by the beauty of his surroundings as the frogs croaking and the crickets chirping made the night come alive. His body was relaxed as his hoodie kept him 72 degrees, yet his skin still registered the low fifties chill of the night.

So, this was the kind of encounter Keith would find: One where he could make a big difference and one where he was sure to win. Was this too specific? Keith quickly put that question of doubt out of his mind. He wasn't sure if it was better to be more specific or less specific in one's beliefs, but he did know that doubt was a no-no.

Keith considered the second half of his problem. If he was going to intervene, then he had to get to this conflict. How? Keith looked at the trees passing him by.

They should change to match the trees of the place he was going.

Keith corrected himself again and instead thought, the trees are changing to match the trees of the place he is going.

Keith walked faster, focusing on this belief of his, on this journey he was taking.

The rocks, the clouds, and the temperature are changing to match the rocks, the clouds, and the temperature of his destination.

Keith kept concentrating and strode purposefully through the forest. Was this going to work? Keith immediately answered that thought with affirmation. Was this whole "go-where-I'm-needed" concept rational? That answer also had to be yes. Keith focused all of his mental discipline to maintain concentration, and just kept running his goals through his mind, over and over.

After a little over 20 minutes of walking, Keith swore that the trees were changing. As soon as Keith started noticing that something was happening, the task became easier, as he no longer needed to doubt its plausibility. Keith began to relax and just let the transformation happen.

The spacing of the trees became wider, and the undergrowth thinned to just a few bushes, making it easier for him to press forward. The ratio of evergreen trees to deciduous trees also appeared to be changing.

Encouraged by these results, Keith increased his focus and kept walking. Soon, there was no doubt about it—the forest was changing around him.

The sounds of the night changed. The number of crickets he could hear increased.

It got warmer, then colder, then warmer again.

The smells of the forest changed so rapidly that it made Keith's head spin. Every three or four paces his nose would be confronted with some new smell, and he barely had enough time to identify the smell before there something new presented itself to his nostrils.

Keith continued walking, fascinated by the positive results of his experiment, yet still absently concentrating on his goal. Though he made sure to never doubt the outcome of his experiment, he couldn't help wondering exactly how it was happening.

Slowly, the changes happening in the forest around him slowed and then seemed to stop altogether. Keith continued walking, not sure exactly what was happening, but confident he was either at or nearing his destination.

The woods looked nothing like the woods Keith had started walking in; the trees were sparse and there were almost no bushes around him. Pines and fir trees were gone, replaced by oaks and hickory trees.

Keith's exposed hands felt slick with moisture. The humidity had gone way up, as had the temperature. Undoubtedly, the biggest change in his environment was the fact that it was getting light out. Keith now realized he had been walking due East, and the changes in the forest seemed to have stopped right when first light had hit him in the face. He wasn't sure how much time had passed since he had started walking, but he was sure he had crossed more than one time zone.

Keith sensed a presence up ahead in the direction of the sun, and he felt pulled towards it. Keith braced himself for the conflict he had chosen to confront, steadied himself with the knowledge that he had chosen a battle in which he would be victorious, and quickened his step. This was his chosen purpose.

As Keith cautiously approached, what he saw was not at all what he was expecting. Rather than some scary, powerful enemy, he saw instead an elderly couple kneeling on the forest floor, face to face, with their hands clasped in front of them. Keith looked around, searching for something more threatening.

Keith approached cautiously. These two did not look like a threat, nor did they look in any way confident.

Noticing Keith, the couple pulled themselves to their feet and turned tired, tear-streaked faces towards him. A man and a woman in their later years, they looked old but tough. The plump woman looked like she had done a lot crying. They watched Keith draw near, expect but silent.

Keith was unsure of how to greet them. He felt no malice, anger, or conflict from these two at all, in fact, he wasn't even sure if they were the reason he was there, or if his experiment had worked. He decided to ask the question foremost on his mind.

"Does, uh … does someone here need me?" Keith ventured as he stopped in front of them.

Both old folks immediately burst into tears and hugged Keith in unison. Keith staggered back, as massive waves of relief from the two hit him. It took a few moments for the old man to get himself under control and extricate himself, but the woman just kept hugging Keith and sobbing. Keith decided he should introduce himself.

"Uh, hi, my name is Keith. Keith Pennison," he began.

"Sorry bouts' that," the old man rubbed his eyes and smiled broadly at Keith. "My name's Tom, Tom Bonner. That precious creature attached to you there is my wife Judy."

Judy managed to smile up at Keith and slightly loosened her grip.

Tom continued, "And yes, my boy. We need you. We need you pretty bad around here."

Day 21

Jacob Christenson was pissed.

Jacob sat on a lawn chair in the parking lot of the still-smoldering church, his gang scattered about. He was exhausted, both physically and mentally, and the sun was approaching its zenith, making the world obnoxiously bright.

The previous evening, when he'd had a nice Preacher Bailey barbeque outside the church, everything seemed to be going smoothly. His minions had commenced their standard reveling in the destruction of the church and all who were inside.

Then it all went to shit.

It had started with a certain lack of enthusiasm in some of his best men. As far back as Bisby, some of his men just didn't seem to have their hearts in the job anymore. Like they were going through the motions, but pillaging somehow wasn't any fun anymore. This seemed odd, but "fun" was such an odd concept to begin with that Jacob hadn't thought much about it.

Then came last night. "Mother fucking Wally," said Jacob under his breath to nobody in particular. A few of his men lounged nearby, but none within earshot.

Wally was a chubby prick who loved to inflict pain on the weak. Wally the brutal, Wally the remorseless, or so was his reputation. Jacob just couldn't believe his eyes when he rounded the back of the church and caught sight of Wally keeping a lookout while church members fled before him.

Jacob had been dumbfounded. Wally, of course, didn't notice he'd been caught, as Jacob began believing long ago that nobody could see him unless he wanted to be seen.

Jacob pressed his hands to his head and massaged his temples. He should have slain Wally on sight for such a betrayal, but the scene was so senseless to Jacob that he had withdrawn to calculate his response. One does not act before understanding the situation. Why was Wally helping them? Did Wally know them? Or did Wally just feel bad for them? Was Wally a Christian? Wally knew full well the price traitors paid. Hell, Wally was usually first in line when such a price needed inflicting. The ramifications of Wally's treachery were tremendously disturbing. If Wally couldn't be trusted, then who could?

Mr. Chuckles came running up to Jacob eagerly.

"Sir, uh, there is a group moving this direction, and, uh, they have a champion, sir."

"Fucking figures," Jacob spat with disgust as he got up. At least he got to take out his frustration on someone. "Thank you, Mr. Chuckles, call the men back to the church, time for yet another barbeque," Jacob sighed, trying to get his anger under control.

"What about, uh, what about …" stammered Chuck.

"What about what, Chuck!? Darrey? What about him?" Jacob exploded. "Yes, that's my question, too. What about Darrey, Chuck?!" Jacob had no idea what Chuck expected of him.

"Uh, nothing boss, I'll go get them right away. Uh, thank you, uh sir," Chuck stammered as he retreated.

Jacob closed his eyes and rubbed his temples again. Darrey was the worst part of the previous evening. Darrey, Jacob's longtime cell mate, Jacob's number one guy, good old Darrey. Fucking Darrey.

Fuck Darrey. Jacob imagined invisible hands grasping Darrey's heart and popping it like a ripe tomato, wherever he was. Then that same thought came to him. Jacob can't find Darrey. Jacob knew this was Darrey's belief, but all his rage and anger at this treachery did nothing to counter it. It only seemed to make it stronger. Such a high-profile betrayal without consequences was inexcusable, and it was having a ripple effect on the rest of Jacob's gang.

As Jacob's men started gathering in a group outside the church, Jacob shook his head and stood up, mentally preparing for the impending fight. It was rare that a champion intentionally approached Jacob looking for trouble, but Jacob cracked his knuckles and welcomed the distraction.

Jacob saw sideways glances and stolen looks as his men fanned out behind him. This wouldn't do. Jacob turned to face his men.

"Anyone else want out? Any more of you fuckwits want to stick a shiv in my back right now?" The Brotherhood stared wide-eyed back at him. His pack needed a morale boost.

"Cause I seem to remember a promise we all made," said Jacob, eyeing the crowd. "And so, I'll ask one last time," said Jacob, scanning the crowd.

"Are you with me!?" Jacob cried.

The crowd cheered back in unison.

"Right!" said Jacob as he turned back around and began walking, his men galvanized behind him, the strength of their wills once again aligned with his.

Jacob began plotting strategies as he moved to meet this challenger, this fool. His decision to confront Jacob would be his last mistake. Jacob was not having a good day, and it would soon be all someone's fault.

Jacob was pissed.

DAY 21

Keith walked towards the church at the front of a small crowd of townsfolk, trying to restrain his fear.

He was their savior, their champion, their knight in shining armor. In addition to the Bonners, many of them had prayed for his arrival, and more than one of them simply believed he would show up. There was no mistaking the reason he was here, though. In their mind, he had one purpose: to kill someone.

"Butterflies in the stomach" did not accurately portray what Keith was feeling. Though he knew he had very intentionally chosen this path, and had placed himself exactly in the line of fire, he couldn't help but feel the urge to tell everyone, "hang on a sec." He wanted to pause and get more information about this Jacob character, he wanted to make sure there was nobody else around who might be a better candidate for the fight, but he knew these things weren't going to happen.

There were about a dozen angry villagers following behind him, pointing him in the direction of the church, where Jacob and his men surely were waiting for him.

Jacob. Jacob, the bloodthirsty marauder with hundreds of willing minions. Jacob, the scourge who sacked the town of Bisby, leaving nothing but burning ruins in his wake. Jacob, the devil king of the Westvale prison, the name that struck fear into the hearts of all who heard it in a hundred-mile radius.

"So, Jacob is real aggressive, right?" Keith asked the crowd, possibly for a second time. Affirmative nods seemed to outnumber the questioning eyes.

"Oh, he's a real fucking bastard," said a tall man with curly hair. This wasn't exactly what Keith had asked. Keith was counting on Jacob making the first move and had been focusing on the belief that Jacob's aggression would not be successful.

Keith calmed his nerves and kept putting one foot in front of the other while reassuring himself. Over the course of a few hours, he had strolled from just outside Seattle to southern Illinois, in pursuit of a challenge that he "could handle." He did not cross the great distance in less time that it would have taken to fly in pursuit of certain death. He was going to be able to handle Jacob, otherwise he wouldn't be here. Right?

Keith tried to review what little he knew about battling powerful adversaries. Lester barely needed a nudge in the direction of his own negative thoughts to panic and flee.

Dealing with a disciplined killer with a cohesive support group was not exactly what Keith was hoping for. Keith wanted more time to practice. He wanted to delay this high-noon face-off, at least for a couple of hours to get his bearings.

But Keith's little posse would have none of it. According to them, Keith was going to put an end to the Jacob menace as soon as humanly or inhumanly possible.

Keith turned over his shoulder and took another look at the small group of townspeople behind him. They were very Midwestern-y, mostly middle-aged white folks, but they all carried an air of anger about them. The night before, Jacob had killed their reverend, among other people, and now the townsfolk were out for blood. They might as well be carrying pitchforks and torches. They seemed to regard Keith as a weird little liberal boy in a hoodie, but they also had absolute and overwhelming faith in him. Keith wasn't quite sure what made all these people so sure that he was going to be the victor in this battle, but he was glad they believed it.

The crowd reached a clearing, and the burnt-out husk of the church came into view. In front of it stood the enemy. There were approximately twenty to thirty men gathered there, and in front of them was Jacob. He was the only one smiling.

Keith stopped walking about forty feet from Jacob as his small group of farmers fell in behind him. As expected, Jacob began.

"So who, exactly, do you think *you* are?" said Jacob as he eyed Keith's unusually heavy outfit.

Before Keith had time to formulate a response, he felt a shove from Jacob. It was not a physical shove, it was more like Jacob just pushed his brain to see what he was dealing with.

This was aggression. And, so, in Keith's mind, this was wrong. Keith's mind didn't budge, but Jacob's thoughts came crashing in like napalm.

Jacob's mind was terrifying. It was full of very controlled hatred, anger, and above all, power. Every thought had a purpose, hierarchical and intentional. Most people's minds were full of contradictions, commotion, and emotions, but Jacob had none of that clutter. Keith wondered exactly what his chances were.

But he could tell something in his own mind had derailed the Jacob train. Keith saw Jacob quickly shake it off and began preparing something fiendish.

"No," stated Keith. His word resonated with his backers. No more of this nonsense.

Once again, Jacob faltered. He was expecting an attack. Then Keith started talking.

"Jacob, you are not wanted here. You have killed many people, corrupted others, and your life is not useful or purposeful in this world."

This attack on Jacob's purpose was once again, not what Jacob or his men expected. Some of Jacob's men shifted uncomfortably. But Jacob held Keith's gaze.

"And?" countered Jacob. "I'm sorry, but I fail to see your point, Mr. Soon-to-be-destroyed." Jacob's face contorted and a fireball of fury began forming in front of him.

"No," said Keith, and the strength of this repeated word dissipated the fireball like mist. Keith was starting to catch the nervous glances of Jacob's men.

"Jacob, we don't like you. Your men don't like you. Nobody likes you. You are not wanted," stated Keith. These accusations were childish, but Keith felt like they needed to be said.

"Aw, now you hurt my feelings. And for that, you must die!" Jacob roared, and Keith felt his body was about to decay. Quickly, even before Jacob finished his sentence, Keith interjected.

"No," was Keith's command that echoed through the forest, as he took a step forward, starting to gain confidence. "Jacob, you are not wanted, you serve no purpose, and you will never change. You are no longer in control here." Keith could tell he hit another nerve with his jab about Jacob's purpose.

"I do not think so, you fuck!" Jacob gnashed, but then his glance caught sight of some of his men, and he seemed to realize the seriousness of his situation.

"Oh no you don't! I am Jacob Christenson! I win all fights. I am feared by everyone, and you are nothing!"

The desperation leaking through Jacob's tirade only encouraged Keith, who got a sad look on his face and took another step towards Jacob.

"I pity you Jacob, I really do. Has anyone ever really cared about you? Did your parents? Do your friends?"

Keith was trying to reference the obviously fractured group, but the mention of Jacob's friends was like touching a live wire. Something about that really bothered Jacob, whose face twisted with rage.

"I don't care!" stammered Jacob. "You are-"

"You are the one who is nothing, Jacob. You hurt and you take, nobody wants you here, and nobody will ever want you anywhere."

The truth of Keith's statements had been resonating with the townsfolk, and were now starting to ring true in the ears of Jacob's men, some of whom began backing away from Jacob.

"It doesn't matter what anyone wants! I ..." Jacob was panicking. "I am Jacob, and I ... I will ..."

"There is only one thing for you to do, only one thing you should do, one thing everyone here wants you to do." Keith paused, melancholy.

Jacob knew he was beaten. Both groups of people were believing every word Keith said. The truth of his words required no deception, no craft, no special delivery. It was obvious to everyone who heard it, including Jacob.

"What?" snarled Jacob, looking at the ground.

At this point, Keith tried to say "go away" or "leave and never come back" or even just "be gone," but his mouth wouldn't work to construct those words. He had never killed anyone and did not want to become a murderer, but he could only say one word. Keith was not in control of the situation either—the crowds were.

With great sadness, Keith said the word that was demanded.

"Die," sighed Keith.

Jacob's lifeless body crumpled to the ground.

MONTH 2

With a mighty "ker-junk," the large yellow school bus careened over the speedbump and sent Jeff Hammond flying. Crashing onto the opposing row of seats inside the speeding yellow rocket, Jeff could not control his own laughter.

"Jesus Christ, Squ- … I mean, Cor!" Jeff corrected himself as he scrambled to his feet and excitedly peeked over the seatbacks at the driver.

"Watch it!" called Cory Nelson, pulling the thin metal steering wheel hand over hand as the bus squealed to the right. "My bad driving won't kill you, but I sure as fuck can!" Cory swore almost as much as Jeff did at this point.

"Sorry, Squeaks," replied Jeff. That bastard.

Cory stomped on the gas pedal and the bus shot forward, launching Jeff to the back of the vehicle. Even though Jeff had become his one and only best friend in the weeks since the world fell apart, he was still an ass.

"You liked that?" Cory taunted. "Then you'll love this!"

Doing somewhere close to 80 mph, Cory yanked the steering wheel hard to his left and kept cranking it. The bus turned, skidded, and rolled.

As the only other passenger, Jeff laughed harder and louder as he was slammed first to the top of the bus as the bus hit its side, then hard to the floor as the bus righted itself. Cory watched Jeff crash around in the back as his seat belt held him tight.

"Off-roading," as he liked to call it, was one of Cory's favorite games. Jeff turned out to be a great sidekick, eager to be by his side every time they failed to die trying something deadly. The Nelson and Hammond parents would probably have had heart attacks if they knew what the kids were up to.

After the bus righted itself and Cory had it suck back and reattach an errant wheel, Cory slammed on the gas again and spun out briefly before resuming their forward momentum.

Cory scanned the horizon for something else that might be fun as the bus picked up speed. Jeff moved up and occupied one of the front seats near Cory.

"Do a jump!" said Jeff.

"Yeah," said Cory thoughtfully. He remembered that one of the bridges that crossed the Hudson had collapsed during the Crack. "A big jump," Cory smiled as he hit the gas and sped towards the river.

After spotting the collapsed bridge and getting their bus on the right road to approach it, the boys prepared for their stunt. But as the ruin came into view more clearly, jumping it seemed less and less practical.

The 199 bridge over the Hudson had simply fallen down during the Crack, leaving two ends of the road angled slightly down into the river. It wasn't exactly a ramp for jumping.

"We're not going to make it!" yelled Jeff, his voice filled with excitement.

"The shit we aren't!" countered Cory, matching Jeff's enthusiasm.

Cory furrowed his brow and large, glowing yellow and red arrows appeared on the road in front of them, right before the road fell into the river. Seeing them, Jeff's eyes went wide as he mumbled with disbelief, "No."

"Yes!" shouted Cory as the bus ran over the arrows.

With a blast, the bus accelerated faster than Old Physics would have allowed, turning into a yellow streak that crossed the entire length of the river with room to spare. With an axle-splitting crash, the bus bounced on the road on the other side of the river and came screeching to a stop, with both boys laughing their pants off.

"You gotta warn me before you go all Mario on my ass again!" howled Jeff.

"I do? That's no fun!" laughed Cory.

Eventually, the boys settled down, pulled their destroyed bus back together, and continued on their way. Youth seemed to have its advantages in this new world. Far more easily than the adults, Cory and Jeff could conjure their reality out of thin air. To them, the rules of the new world were not that much different than the rules of the old; they were just about ten times more fun.

MONTH 7

Keith Pennison stepped through the broken front door of the Admiral Theater in West Seattle. Once inside the lobby, the stylish mid-century lighting fixtures flickered to life around him. All electric grids had gone down long ago, but that didn't stop everyone's personal lighting effects.

Keith had been thinking.

After the whole Jacob incident, Keith had "gone where he was needed" a few more times, but quickly realized that even though he could probably do the most good that way, battling and killing was simply not how he wanted to spend his time. He had concluded that what he wanted to do more than help people was to understand more about the new universe that he lived in.

Keith made his way through the hallways of the theater, followed by his lighting. Finally, he went through a thick door with a metal handle and found himself in an empty theater with stale air, as the lights inside flickered on, which included a powerful projector bulb. Keith flipped that one off.

Sitting down in the back row, Keith began focusing on his task.

He wanted a teacher. Not like Rupert; he had no time for riddles, plus Rupert probably wouldn't think helping Keith was worth his time. Not that Orange Chick, her voluptuousness would only be too distracting. This teacher would be easily understood, friendly, and helpful. Keith concentrated. This teacher would appear next to him.

It took about five seconds.

Suddenly there was a pop, and in the chair next to Keith sat a young boy. Immediately the boy jumped up and stood on his theater chair and shouted, "it worked!"

Keith was shocked by the boy's age. He couldn't be more than thirteen. Blond hair. Pre-pubescent, definitely. This was his teacher?

"Hey there, uh…" Keith wasn't used to dealing with children, and he wasn't even sure what he should say to this boy. "Bud?"

Fortunately, the boy was quite comfortable dealing with adults. He turned, saw Keith, and then jumped down and stuck out his hand.

"Cory Nelson's my name, don't wear it out!" said Cory, smiling.

"Hey, uh, my name is Keith," replied Keith.

"So, what do you want? You just wanted me for something. I've been trying teleportation, but all I ever go is where someone wants me. I haven't been able to go where I want … yet …" Cory mused as he walked down the aisle away from Keith.

"Well, uh, I was hoping for someone to clear some stuff up for me," Keith reevaluated the boy. He sure didn't look like he knew anything.

"Okay, go for it!" Cory sat in mid air, crossing his legs underneath him and spinning around, turning back to Keith.

"Well, do you know what happened to the world?" Keith felt this was a good start.

"What do you mean? Belief is real, two beats one, circle beats squares," stated Cory.

"Right, yeah, I guess I meant how did it happen," Keith rephrased.

"How does all life happen?" Cory said, as he inverted himself into a handstand, walking on the backs of the seats, upside down without any blood rushing to his head. "Evolution, of course. Don't you think mind powers would give you an edge on your neighbor?" asked Cory as he righted himself standing on a seat in the center of the theater. "Of course, when everyone started believing in their believing, things kinda snowballed," he said.

"What do you mean?" asked Keith. Cory furrowed his little brow.

"Have you heard of 'The Secret' or maybe the 'Law of Attraction'?" asked Cory. "How about the 'Power of Prayer,' or even maybe the 'Placebo Effect?'"

"Sort of," Keith said hesitantly. He was pretty sure he knew the basics of all of those things, but he was never into any New Age stuff before the Crack.

"Really? I haven't," laughed Cory. "You must think I know stuff."

"What?" asked Keith. He's the one who brought them up. This kid was wacky.

"So before, these things were real, but nobody believed in them much," Cory said, ignoring Keith. "But the more they became more real, the more people believed, and, well, you know—snowball."

"Wow," said Keith, thinking about how long those concepts had been a part of history. "So, you're saying the Crack was inevitable?"

"How would I know?" laughed Cory. "I'm just a kid!" Cory stood up on a seat in front of Keith and crossed his arms, suddenly deep in thought. "Then again, I sure do wish I knew more stuff like old people. So let me talk out my ass some more," Cory said as he snuck a smiling glance at Keith's face. "I mean, talk out of my butt."

"So let me get this straight," interrupted Keith. "When everyone suddenly believed in David Archer's 'everyone can do it' line at once, everyone who saw the effect believed in it too and magnified it?"

"Yup," said Cory, as he walked away from Keith again. He suddenly looked disinterested. "Good thing David Archer didn't say anything scarier like 'everyone has two heads,' or 'the world is ending.'"

As scary as these possibilities were, the amount of death and destruction caused by the Crack was not exactly insignificant. "Boy, I wish there was some way we could somehow go back in time and warn everyone," Keith said.

A smile flashed across Cory's face as he whirled around to face Keith. "You mean, go back and tell everyone that everything will be okay? That everything is getting better? That their tractor will start? That they are the best cook in town? Believe that the bully won't see you when you walk by? That the monster under the bed is not real?"

These were strangely specific examples.

"Well, yeah, stuff like that, sure," said Keith.

"Naw," said Cory, turning away and walking out the door grinning. "That's impossible."